RELICT

D.T. NEAL
RELICT

CHICAGO | PITTSBURGH

Relict
© 2013 by D. T. Neal. All Rights Reserved.

ISBN-13: 978-1482741872

Published by Nosetouch Press
www.nosetouchpress.com

This book is a work of fiction. Names, characters, places, and incidents either are products of the author's imagination or are used fictitiously. Any resemblance to actual persons, living or dead, events, or locales is entirely coincidental.

Publisher's Note:
No part of this publication may be reproduced, distributed, or transmitted in any form or by any means, including photocopying, recording, or other electronic or mechanical methods, without the prior written permission of the publisher, except in the case of brief quotations embodied in critical reviews and certain other noncommercial uses permitted by copyright law.

For more information about bulk purchases,
please contact Nosetouch Press at info@nosetouchpress.com.

Cataloging-in-Publication Data

Names: Neal, D.T., author.
Title: Relict / D.T. Neal
Description: Chicago, IL : Nosetouch Press [2013]
Identifiers: ISBN: 9781482741872 (paperback)
Subjects: LCSH: Horror—Fiction. | Sea monsters—Fiction. | GSAFD: Horror fiction. | BISAC: FICTION / Horror.

Cover & interior designed by
Christine M. Scott, Clever Crow Consulting and Design
www.clevercrow.com

The text for this book was set in Minion Pro.

For Paige,
wherever she may be.

ONE

OVERCAST skies painted the jungle black. Great rainclouds loomed and desultory drizzle fell as the ketch, *Affinity*, cruised toward Palmer Atoll, a coral comma that punctuated the middle of the Pacific Ocean.

Aboard her were Margaret "Meg" Trumbo, and her husband, Sebastian. Meg perched at the bow, catching the breeze in her white swimsuit, her black hair held back by a slender white band, great sunglasses on her face. Sebastian was tanned and white-haired, sure-handed on the wheel, eyes bleached pale by countless cruises.

John Marsden and his girlfriend, Paige Wilkins, rounded out the crew of *Affinity*, with Marsden topside, watching the approaching atoll, and Paige belowdecks, trying to shake off a stubborn cold.

Marsden was Sebastian's protégé at Titan Electric Boat, well-schooled in hydrodynamics, ergonomics, and economics. Their goal was to craft sailboats that relied on vertical turbines that would catch the wind and generate power, could move capably and quickly across any seas.

Affinity was one of their prototypes: this was her maiden voyage, and she carried ample batteries down below for reserve power, while twin columns of spinning white—polycarbonate vertical turbines—caught and claimed the wind for their own, channeling power throughout the ship.

"Not the same as sails, I know," Sebastian said, tugging down his navy blue and white Titan Electric Boat ballcap. "Not half the romance, but twice the power. Twice the power."

"What happens if they break?" Paige said, coming up from below.

The air was still warm after the last rain. Her blonde hair was cut short in a pixie-like shag, her eyes were hazel, her smile crooked. The antihistamine was kicking in, and she was feeling human again.

She hadn't smiled since Hilo, when the cold had hit her shortly after they'd shipped out, cruising smoothly whichever way they pleased, as *Affinity* could ride with or tack against the wind. Tourist and yachties alike had marveled at her lean, sleek white frame, the twin poles doing endless pirouettes, whirling like dervishes.

Paige had liked their looks of wonder as *Affinity* had made her way, cutting through the currents. She'd waved at the onlookers, and they'd waved back; Paige felt like maritime royalty. Now she just felt like shit, her head had been throbbing, nose red, cheeks flushed. She thought maybe she had a fever, which made this worse than a simple cold, but the drugs were at least beginning to work their medicinal magic.

John nodded as she came up, then watched the turbines whirl almost silently, then turned his gaze back to Palmer.

"If they break," John said. "We have enough stored power for days. From where we're at, we can reach Johnston Atoll, Kingman Reef and Palmyra Atoll, or Howland Island, if we had to. In a pinch, we might even make Majuro, on the Marshall Islands, if you're yearning for civilization."

John took out his digital camera, snapped a picture of Palmer Atoll. He had taken dozens of pictures already on their cruise.

"Not so much on Howland," Sebastian said, with a wink. "A lot of nothing. Amelia Earhart was supposed to get there, and she never made it. Just a lot of birdshit."

"Then what are we doing out here?" Paige asked, wiping her nose with the back of her hand.

"Palmer," Sebastian said, nodding. "That's why we're here."

Paige squinted and hooded her eyes with her hand. Even with the thick carpet of clouds overhead, the light was still bright to her eyes, accustomed as they were to Portland. She'd met John there while kayaking. His veiled, almost apologetic brilliance had enticed and intoxicated her.

"It looks like nothing," Paige said.

"Just trees," John said, smiling at her. "Palm trees, that's all. It's only paradise."

"Palmer trees," Paige said under her breath.

Paige knew nothing about islands, where they were and weren't, why one was an atoll, why another was something else. She had liked Hawaii. It was large and lush, alive, active, and big enough that she felt comfortable upon it. She loved the volcanic Big Island. Mountains made her feel welcome. It felt good to look out at them, see them lurking in the background, like gentle giants.

But this place barely stood over the sea. It looked like a good wave would just wash right over it, like a drowning person treading water, losing strength, their mouth all that remained above the water, one last geographic gasp before the ocean claimed it.

"The Navy never made use of it," Sebastian said. "Nobody had any use for it. Maybe the Japanese, during the War, but after that, nothing. Tricky reefs, bad currents."

Sebastian spun the wheel, and *Affinity* turned hard to port.

"It's like an iceberg, in a way," he said. "The reefs surround what's left of the island. It will be a seamount soon enough."

He pointed as *Affinity* turned, and Paige could see the lighter blue of the shallows, filled with coral and fish. It was beautiful and haunting, with the indigo hue of the deeps just beyond it.

"Ships come in all the time on these, come crashing onto the shallows, get themselves stuck, or sunk," Sebastian said. "You have to pay attention."

Paige watched the sailboat slide smoothly alongside the reefs. She could see a tapestry of color and life in the water. Turtles, sharks, eels, fish of every shape and size.

"It's beautiful," she said.

"Sure is," John said.

Meg walked down from the bow, having tied a shawl around her midsection. She treated them to a glamorous, accommodating smile as she walked past John and Paige, settled in beside Sebastian.

RELICT

"There's a way into the lagoon on the southwest side," Sebastian said. "You have to go slowly, though; it's not very roomy."

"Why haven't people settled here?" John asked. He kept an ear out for the turbines, gauging their performance as he had for the duration of their cruise.

"Who says they haven't?" Sebastian said. He nodded to a weatherbeaten sign indicating "Palmer Atoll. 10° 28' N 170° 07' W. Population 01. Elevation 5.2 feet. DANGER! KEEP OFF!"

Paige shuddered at the sight of the sign, all rust and salt spray and peeling paint. The number 1 looked relatively recent, a thin metal plaque that hung from a rusty hook. The island's elevation was shorter than she was. The warning was hastily spray-painted in red, a half-hearted skull and crossbones rendered that made the skull look like it had a dreadlocked beard, several tendrils dripping down from the mouth.

"Does it have fresh water?" she asked.

"Some of these atolls have a freshwater lens," John said. "Usually inhabitants put containers up to catch rainwater. It rains a lot down here, so there's usually plenty that way."

"Are we having fun yet?" Meg asked, smiling radiantly. Paige admired her grace, hoped she'd have as much effortless elegance as Meg Trumbo had, when her time came. She was probably ten years older than Paige, maybe more, but looked great. But then, she was a statuesque 5'11", and had room to spare for grace; at 5'5", Paige felt shrimplike by comparison.

"Who do you think lives here?" John asked. Sebastian shrugged.

"Could be anybody," he said. "Vagrants, castaways. A caretaker, even."

"It's not a private island, is it?" John asked. Sebastian shook his head. His eyes were on the lagoon, on the channel that led to it. He slowed *Affinity* down.

"It won't be here much longer," Sebastian said. "As the sea levels rise, places like these will just become navigation hazards."

The lagoon was deep and dark, as dark as the ocean around Palmer Atoll, and Sebastian slid *Affinity* between the pincerlike shoals of the island that screened it.

"One good storm could clear it out, seems like," Paige said. "Right?"

"I don't know," John said. "Out here? I don't know."

It frightened Paige to see this little sliver of land in the middle of absolutely nowhere, surrounded by the deepest, darkest sea and an endless sky—cloudy today, but as overpowering as it was on a clear day, too. It made her short of breath, made her grip the railing of the ketch. For an asthmatic, being short of breath was a familiar feeling. She took a puff of her inhaler. The cold or flu had made everything worse, as it always did with asthma.

"There aren't any proper ports here," Sebastian said. "But we can anchor in the lagoon, then take a dinghy to the shore."

Paige fought for breath, the tightness in her chest compounded by the bug she had, making breathing a battle. The asthma medication worked, though, and she felt her breath come easier.

"You okay?" John asked. She nodded, took another puff on her inhaler.

"Who would live here?" she asked. "I mean it. Who could stand it?"

"Somebody who likes getting away from it all," Meg said, smiling languidly, lounging just past Sebastian's elbow.

Palmer was beautiful, the pinkish-white coral sands, the palm trees in intermittent clumps and groves, the brush the color of jade, although in the thick clouds, the colors were dulled and muted. It didn't look like paradise to her; it looked like purgatory. She peeked over the railing, into the depths of the lagoon, dark as ink. It looked like death.

"How deep is it?" Paige asked, gazing into the eye of the lagoon, lidless and unblinking, like a shark's eye.

"Who knows?" Sebastian said. "Usually lagoons are fairly shallow, but Palmer was once a volcano, long, long ago, and those tend to go very deep."

He pulled *Affinity* along the shore, until he reached a proper anchorage. He brought her to a stop, smiled at John.

"She's sailing beautifully, John," Sebastian said. "Just a peach."

John eyed the turbines, which now settled a bit that they were partially screened by the far side of Palmer Atoll, where the trees rustled and caught the breeze. Now the turbines looked almost like great wind chimes, sliding this way and that. He was very proud of the boat, of what she'd accomplished, of what it would mean for his future, and the future of Titan Electric Boat.

"I hope to take her back to Hilo," John said.

Sebastian nodded.

"Sure, sure," he said. "Everybody can take a turn at the wheel, once we're out of here."

There was a corrugated tin shack on one side of the lagoon, near the upswell of trees, and a couple of cisterns standing on rusting, spindly legs. Piled beside the shack like bones was plastic of all shapes and sizes, sunbleached. Bottles, mostly, but also netting, and other things. Cigarette lighters in great stacks, separated by color: red, yellow, blue, green, purple, and orange, a great mound of them.

"Wow," Paige said. "Look at all of that junk."

"Enough isobutane for a generation," John said.

"You'd be amazed what washes up on these remote islands," Sebastian said. "The litter is carried by the currents. There are some places out there where there is just this great swirling mass of plastic garbage, floating out there—a Sargasso Sea of plastics."

"Sounds lovely," Meg said.

"People are pigs," Paige said, transfixed by all the garbage somebody had neatly arranged by the ramshackle hut. There was an old hibachi nearby, and a tin washtub hanging from a hook on one of the posts.

"Headhunters used to call people 'long pig,'" John said. "That was their name for us. I mean, for their prey."

Paige wrinkled her brow at the thought. "Gross."

"Yes," Meg said. "I've got a picnic basket belowdecks. Why don't I get that ready?"

Meg disappeared below, while Paige lurked on deck with John, who reached out and touched the turbines, ran his hand across them.

"Just beautiful," he said. "We did it, Sebastian."

Sebastian let loose the anchor, smiled at his passengers. "The dinghy's aft. We can take it ashore, once we're ready."

Paige put on her sunglasses, despite the clouds, and stared at the shack. The heat was unbelievable. After being in the air-conditioned confines of the cabin below, to stand in the heavy, humid air was almost too much to bear. And even with her cold, she could smell the ocean, the salty, fishy scent, and other smells, hints of plants she could not identify. And other things.

"Ahoy!" she yelled. "Anybody home?"

It felt rude, somehow, to do otherwise, to just come ashore in this place. Somebody lived here. This was their home, or their tomb. It hardly looked like anybody could live in this place, at least as she understood living.

John patted her arm, smiled in a way that felt patronizing. "I'm sure they know we've come. They'd have seen us coming for miles, if they were paying attention."

Meg emerged with a basket, which she handed over to John. Despite her misgivings about the place, the remnants of her fever, cold, or whatever it was, after days at sea, Paige looked forward to setting foot on land, even as inconsequential land as this was.

Sebastian lowered the dinghy, and gestured to the rope ladder. Meg went down first, then Paige. John handed down the picnic basket, then went down, himself.

Once everybody was settled, Sebastian fired up the little motor and the dinghy cruised ashore. After being cooped up on *Affinity*, Paige felt exposed in the tiny dinghy, felt more vulnerable than ever. To her right, the palm trees swayed in the breeze. To the left, the far arm of the atoll, curving, just barely above the surf, a long arm of sand and crushed coral, upon which crabs crawled, between clusters of palms.

"Where are the birds?" Paige asked. "Shouldn't there be birds?"

"Probably not the right time of year," John said. "Migratory birds and all of that."

Sebastian turned off the motor, threw a line and jumped into the water, tied down the dinghy. The others followed.

"I don't know if migratory birds head this way," Sebastian said. "There are easier hauls for them than Palmer. Although I could be wrong; it happens now and then."

"When did you first discover this place?" John asked.

"Just recently," Sebastian said. "It's not on most charts. A friend of mine told me about it. Told me to stay the hell away from it, in fact. Said it was a bad place."

"A bad place?" Paige asked. Sebastian nodded.

"You lose your ship out here, and you've vanished from the face of the Earth. It's not on prime shipping lanes. It is between them, in fact. You lose it out here, and that's it. Nobody is ever going to find you."

"And so you took us here why?" Paige asked.

"For fun," Sebastian said, smiling. "Look, when a yachtie says 'stay away' from someplace, that's like waving a cape before the bull, at least it is for me. Then I just had to see it. It usually means there's something worth seeing here."

Despite her initial enthusiasm, Paige found the ground unfamiliar beneath her feet, so accustomed to sailing she'd come since Portland. *Affinity* had sailed from there to Hawaii in record time, to much fanfare from the Titan Electric Boat people, who had seen them off with cheers and gusty celebrations.

There was no sound but the waves and the wind, and the noise they brought with them, John's steady speaking rhythm, Sebastian's staccato delivery, Meg's languorous tone, and the clatter of them walking toward the shack, which stood empty, without walls. Just a tin roof with four posts upon it, and the sorted piles of debris.

Paige knelt to inspect some of the lighters. The metal parts were rusted, although many of them were nearly full. She turned one in her hands. A green one. Over and over, tried to spark the flint, but the wheel wouldn't turn. She tossed it back into the pile.

"Island fever," John said. "What else is there to do around here except go crazy, I guess?"

From where they stood, they could walk from one side of the beach to the other in about a dozen paces. On the far side was a ton of litter on the beach, bobbing up and down with the surf, which pushed the junk ashore. Paige pointed to it, and John shrugged, while Meg and Sebastian set up in the shack.

"Where do you think the resident is?" Paige asked.

"Maybe out collecting food," John said.

"Maybe hiding," Paige said. "Maybe watching."

"Headhunters," John said, mock-grinning at Paige, who half-heartedly rapped him on the shoulder.

She looked at the tall palms, waving breezily. Anybody could've been in there.

"We'll have our picnic and then explore the atoll," Sebastian said. "We can watch the sunset and then get back to *Affinity*, spend the night, and then head back to Hawaii, if you'd like. We can do absolutely anything we want."

Paige hadn't thought about what they were going to do. The goal had been merely to reach Palmer Atoll; she hadn't really thought past it. The idea of spending the night at this place made her afraid. She clutched herself, shivered. John patted her back.

"What's wrong, Paige?" he asked.

"I don't like this place," she said. "It's just off."

She couldn't put her finger on it, either. It was just wrong. Meg looked up from her picnic preparations, and Sebastian smiled.

"People sometimes get disturbed by little islands," Sebastian said. "It happens."

"No," Paige said. "There's just something wrong here. Something is not right about this place. Can't you feel it?"

Meg had laid out a blanket, a bottle of chilled Dom Perignon, some crusty bread and soft cheese and tins of meat and caviar. She paused to look up at Paige.

"How do you mean, Paige?" she asked.

"It's just a vibe," Paige said. She couldn't quite define it, herself, and she was feeling it. As her eyes raked the forlorn and litter-strewn shore, panned across the thick little jungle, there was just this sense of Palmer Atoll being a place that didn't want people on it. The clouds broke and revealed blue sky, letting beams of sunlight through, illuminating the water around them, making the beach sparkle.

"Everything's better in the sun," Meg said, smiling. "The sun makes everything tolerable. Even bad things are tolerable in sunlight."

Paige looked around the shack. There wasn't even a bench or a bed, a place for somebody to sleep. Did the dweller sleep on the ground? Really, the place didn't look like it had been inhabited recently. It looked abandoned, weatherbeaten.

"Somebody stacked this stuff up," Paige said, pointing to the debris. "But it looks like they haven't done it for awhile, judging from the beach on the far side."

"Maybe they just gave up," John said. "It's like sweeping back the sea; you just can't do it."

"We should clean this place up," Paige said, more to herself than to the others, since none of them appeared eager to do that.

"Not our job," Sebastian said. "We're here to recreate."

Paige sighed. Nobody would get it. She'd just look paranoid if she kept going on about it, but she knew in her heart that something was wrong with this place; she just didn't know what was wrong.

"Let's just have our picnic and then go for a stroll around," Sebastian said. "We can't come all this way and not look around, can we? If the caretaker is here, we'll ask him to join us."

Paige joined Meg at the picnic blanket. Meg had Sebastian pop the champagne and they poured some for each of them. It was marvelously chilled, felt heavenly in the hot, thick, tropical air.

"To paradise," Sebastian said. "Lost, found, whatever."

They all drank, Paige drinking in the details of the island as she drank down the excellent champagne. *Affinity* had a refrigerator on board, one of the amenities offered by the copious power reserves of the boat. It had been one of the pleasant surprises of the cruise, another demonstration of the superior design of the ketch.

The sun dipped back behind a layer of clouds, and another rain started to fall, hitting the tin roof with big drops the size of marbles.

"Your friend said it was a bad place, Sebastian," Paige said.

Sebastian watched her with the narrowest of smiles. "That he did."

"Why? Bad how?" Paige asked.

"Oh, you know, the usual thing," Sebastian said. "Ships lost. Crashed upon the shoals and reefs, people lost at sea. That kind of thing. But it's beautiful. Almost nobody has been here. That's what matters. The absence of civilization, except for us, of course."

"And the litter," Meg said. "Is litter a sign of civilization or barbarity, I wonder?"

Paige perked up, looked around, discovered what had been bothering her. "Where's the caretaker's ship? All I see is a little kayak over there."

There was a clear-hulled kayak covered in dust, in the far side of the shack. Paige couldn't imagine that thing traveling across the ocean.

"Maybe a castaway, then," John said, looking around. Meg smiled a little uncomfortably, and even Sebastian looked around, if only for a moment.

"Maybe they're gone," Meg said, between sips of champagne.

"Maybe they're dead," Paige said. Her head was aching. She wondered if the antihistamine would mix well with the champagne, or badly. Probably badly, knowing her luck. Maybe it was the absence of the boat that bothered her, fed the feeling of wrongness, that feeling of being exposed.

"Silly Paige," John said. "Someone left and forgot to change the number on the sign."

They ate and drank in the rain, sheltered in the shack, waiting for the appearance of the caretaker, who never came. Paige felt dizzy from the alcohol, hyper-aware of everything around them. The way the posts of the shack looked like driftwood. The patter of the rain, the sonorous crashing of the waves. The soothing whir of the wind—all conspired to both charm and alarm Paige. And beyond that, the breezy silence of the place.

"It is beautiful, Sebastian," Meg said. "I'm so glad you took us here."

From where they sat, their backs to the far side of the atoll, the litter couldn't be seen. Just the depths of the lagoon, sheltered from the wind and waves, and *Affinity*.

"After our picnic, we'll walk into the jungle," John said. "Have a look around."

"'Jungle' seems rather generous for that little grove," Meg said. "I hope there aren't mosquitoes."

"Usually there aren't," Sebastian said. "They have to be brought to a place like this. They're lazy fliers, mosquitoes. We're too far for them."

"Wonderful," Meg said. "Oh, look."

A coconut crab toddled toward them, a great big thing, reddish-brownish. Big claws gripping the ground.

"Massive," Sebastian said.

John took out his digital camera, snapped a picture of it. The crab kept scuttling toward them, moving slowly.

"Freeloader," Sebastian said, tossing a cracker at it. The cracker bounced off the crab's carapace, landed on the beach behind it. It was amazing to Paige that the beach was so close to them. The water just wasn't ever far away here.

The crab went after the cracker, stalking over to it and crushing it in its pincers, bringing up little bits of it to its mouthparts. Watching it, Paige realized just how many crabs there were on Palmer Atoll. They were everywhere, squirming. It was the kind of thing that she noticed more the more she looked—the more she looked, the more she saw.

"I heard somewhere that one time a man was killed by a coconut crab because he slept on the ground, and the crab thought his head was a coconut, and it crushed his skull with its claw," John said, winking at Paige, who grimaced at the thought of it. The crab was huge. It was the largest, most horrible creepy-crawly she'd ever seen. It looked like an alien, like a great spider.

"Nonsense," Sebastian said. "A fairy tale."

"What I heard," John said, shrugging, having more champagne.

"I wonder how they taste," Meg said. "I mean, if they dine on coconuts, they must taste like them, yes?"

"They're supposed to be delicious," John said. "Great big hermit crabs."

"They also call them Robber Crabs," Sebastian said. "They will steal things if they can. Watch."

The crab finished with the cracker, then again crept toward their picnic blanket. The rain had made its carapace shiny. Sebastian took a fork and tossed it near the crab. To the delight of the others, the crab took up the fork in its claw, working it this way and that, turning it, examining it.

John took his camera and clicked off some pictures of the crab brandishing the fork. "Now that's an image—a crab with a fork in its claw, ready to dine!"

The crab crept away with its prize, moving in that creeping kind of way that greatly unnerved Paige.

"Nasty," she said. "Horrible."

"Beautiful," Sebastian said. "Island ecosystems at work. They must be the dominant predator on the island, obviously. Only in isolated places like this can you have a crab at the apex of the food pyramid. Can you imagine? Great big hermit crabs, ruling their islands?"

"I thought it was a food chain," John said.

"Chains are so binding," Sebastian said. "A pyramid gives you something to aspire to, a place to go. Chains are for slaves, webs are for prey. A pyramid, though—that is something altogether grander. Put me atop a food pyramid, and I'm a happy man. This atoll is a pyramid, of sorts, leading all the way to the bottom of the sea. We are at the pinnacle."

"With an army of worshipful appetizers below, no doubt," Meg said, grinning at her man.

Paige watched the crab make its way along the shore, then returned her attention to the others. John and Sebastian were talking about islands, while Meg nipped at her caviar and crackers, sipped her champagne, inscrutable as a sphinx behind her great sunglasses.

Then Paige looked up and saw a long, thick, snakelike thing slip out of the water and snatch up the coconut crab, coil around it, and yank the crustacean into the water with barely a splash. It was greenish-black in color, smooth and horrible and dreadfully long, like a mass of tubing, like a flexible tree or pipe. She gasped, jumped to her feet, pointing, words failing her.

The others turned and looked, but there was nothing to see. Just the lagoon, the angular pinkish shore, the rustling of the crabs. But not the crab with the fork. Both the crab and the fork were gone.

"What is it?" John asked.

"Something just snatched up the crab," Paige said. "Like a snake."

"Impossible," Sebastian said. "No snakes out here. Sea snakes, maybe, but they're in the water; they take prey in the water."

"I saw it," Paige said. "Maybe a tentacle. I don't know. Something."

John went over to where the crab had been. "Over here?"

Paige nodded.

"Crabs have burrows, I think," Sebastian said. "It probably went to its hiding place."

"I saw it," Paige said. "Something snatched it up, took it away."

She held a finger up, hooked it, while the others looked at her. It was frustrating, because she didn't know what she'd seen, exactly. An octopus? A squid?

"A tentacle," she said. "It was a tentacle. Like a long, thick tube. It grabbed the crab."

"We'd have heard a splash," Sebastian said. "Some kind of noise, at the very least."

It was infuriating to her. Of course their backs had been to it, of course she'd been the only one to see it. John paced back and forth at the spot where the crab had been taken, his shoes crunching on the coral sand.

The crab, which had seemed so large to Paige, had looked like a little squeeze toy in the grip of the thing, which had wrapped itself tight around the crab and flung it up, then had slipped back into the water without a sound. Her mind recalled the details in afterimages that played in her head, over and over. The glint of the fork held in the crab's claw. It hadn't even had time to drop its little trinket, before it had been taken. The slickness of the surface of the tentacle, the alien smoothness of it. It was a tentacle; she was sure of it.

"I don't see anything," John said, leaning forward, looking into the lagoon.

"We should get out of here," Paige said. "Right now."

John laughed. "We just got here, Paige."

"Right fucking now," Paige said.

"You don't want to tour the atoll?" John said. "It's not that big."

"Fuck the atoll," Paige said. "Sebastian, would you take me back to *Affinity*?"

The older man looked at his wife a moment, a glance exchanged, just a momentary, intimate thing.

Paige didn't care if they thought she was crazy; she didn't care. She saw what she saw. Sebastian pursed his lips, took a moment before replying.

"If that thing you saw was real, Paige," Sebastian said. "It's in the water, isn't it? That dinghy would hardly be protection from it. No protection at all. What's to say it won't come back? Why don't we just wait for it to move on?"

The thought of the thing grabbing her in the boat made Paige all the more afraid, made her hands sweat, made her mouth dry. The champagne was forgotten, then; it was just a touch of sourness in her mouth, the alcohol an acid burn in her belly.

"Paige, darling," Meg said. "Why don't we let the boys explore, and we can just wait here by the shack, sheltered from the rain? There's plenty of champagne handy."

Meg nodded to the bottle, which sat in its bucket of melting ice, while rain pattered on the ground. It looked like it was going to stop. Maybe the sound of the rain falling had disguised the sound of the horrible thing. Maybe the sound of the surf. Maybe she had imagined it.

No, it was real; she'd seen it.

Meg saw the looks crossing Paige's face, saw her working it out in her head, mistook it for compliance. "We can stay dry, let John and Sebastian get all damp and scratched by the jungle bushes as they play safari explorers. We can have our luncheon and just relax. If the sun comes out, we might even get a little tan."

She could see from the others' faces that they wanted her to go along with them, maybe needed it. It was that kind of vibe that could come out on long trips like that, confined on something like a ship, or a car. Just anything to keep the noise down. That was what they wanted.

"Okay," Paige said, against her better instincts. "We can wait here."

She felt like an automaton, going against what she knew she had seen, what she wanted to do. She looked at *Affinity*, floating there, maybe 50 yards away, a world away. Safety. Sanctuary. She thought the thing couldn't sink that. Paige needed to think that. The alternative was just too terrible.

The shack, the whole atoll, felt impossibly small. The ocean lapped at them from either side. Could the thing reach them? Nothing felt safe to her. She found it hard to breathe, but didn't want another shot of her inhaler. She had to keep calm.

More of the crabs crawled about, nearing their camp. She'd never seen so many crabs. They made her skin itch, with all of those legs, the way they moved. She'd eaten crab so often in her life, but to see those thick legs moving, it was just too much.

"If it was a thing," Meg said. "Maybe it just loves crabs. Maybe it's a natural predator of them."

"Octopi love crabs," John said. "If it was an octopus, maybe it just wanted a crab."

Paige wasn't so sure. She didn't know anything about octopi, but they lived in the water. She couldn't imagine one hunting outside of water. Then again, the crab was near the shore.

"It was big," Paige said.

"The water plays tricks on the eyes," John said.

"It wasn't in the water," Paige said. "It was out of the water. One big-ass tentacle, John."

John looked at her like he was embarrassed, her making an issue of it in front of Sebastian.

Sebastian looked skyward. "I'd wager we have a few hours until sunset. We simply have to catch the sunset. Sunsets out in the Pacific are glorious things."

"Fine," John said, looking at Paige. "We'll walk around, look for buried treasure."

Paige wouldn't turn her back on the lagoon, glowered at John. But the atoll was so small, it meant turning her back on the ocean, to face the lagoon. Which was the bigger menace? It seemed absurd. Maybe she'd become agoraphobic after their long cruise. She'd found the open space of Palmer almost intolerable. There was nothing around them. Nothing but the sea. Nothing but that thing in the water.

"It's settled, then," Sebastian said. "You ladies can stay here, and John and I will reconnoiter. If we see any snakes or sea serpents, we'll holler."

Sebastian readjusted his cap, nodded to John, and the two of them went walking toward the strip of jungle. It didn't even seem right to Paige to call that green-black patch a jungle. There wasn't enough of it to merit jungle status. To her, jungles should be trackless and unimaginably vast. But this grove looked more like a desert oasis, a beckoning finger of foliage on a massive, inky sea. The color of the plants reminded her of the thing in the water, and she shivered.

Meg was watching her, smiling politely, uncomprehending. Paige thought she looked a little like Sela Ward, could see that gracious radiance about her as she sought to soothe Paige, who was still upset about what she'd seen.

"I'm sure it was nothing for us to worry about. One time Sebastian took me out on one of his boats, and we got caught in a hurricane. That was a frightening trip. I've never felt closer to death than in a storm like that. But Sebastian insisted that we ride it out. It wasn't like we had much choice in the matter. He was sure his boat would survive it, although I was petrified. I trusted him, and we survived it."

"If you'd only seen the thing," Paige said. "It was dreadful."

She watched the men walking along the rocky rim of the lagoon, getting smaller.

"I'm sure it seemed that way," Meg said. "But we're up here, and it's down there, whatever it was."

Paige looked back at the lagoon, which was almost still, now, just a slight ebb and flow to the dark waters, contrasted with the churning surf of the open ocean against the outer banks of the atoll, smashing and crashing. The violence of it was extraordinary, the relentlessness of the assault. How any island could live in the wake of such an endless onslaught gave Paige pause. Even the greatest island would one day be drowned by the sea.

"Once we're back on *Affinity*, then where?" Paige asked. "Where is Sebastian taking us?"

"Back to Hilo," Meg said. "I think that was the plan, although he's a wanderer, you know; he loves playing with his boats, and this one, oh my, he just absolutely adores it."

Paige kept her eyes on the lagoon.

It was in there, that thing.

She knew it.

But it couldn't see them, not from in the water.

She looked at John and Sebastian, who were now barely visible, having tramped into the jungle. She just saw John's head a moment, bobbing in the brush, and the flash of color of Sebastian's cap, white and blue, and then gone amid the sullen green of the jungle.

"We're all alone," Paige said. "They've abandoned us."

Meg laughed, soft and lilting, knowing. "Chivalry is long dead, you know. All the knights have fallen into rust and ruin. We're on our own."

Paige had this image of knights in their armor, drowning in the bottom of the sea, and shivered. Everything was making her think of death and drowning. She imagined piles of crab carcasses, empty shells sucked clean, piled beneath the crystalline water, and skulls and bones of countless victims of the thing, carefully arranged.

An octopus's garden in the bottom of the lagoon, an oceanic ossuary placed there by that thing. The ocean was a giant graveyard, Paige thought, full of all the things that had died within its depths.

She'd never really thought of it back home; she loved the ocean, loved the coast. But there was, in her mind, a distinction between the comfort of the coast, and being here, in this place, far from everything, away from the world. There was no comfort here, only loneliness, emptiness, and lurking fear. She could not deny it. It was different in the boat, because the boat was going places, could travel the world—here, there was no place to go.

"The rain stopped," Meg said. "Finally."

She poured herself some more champagne, and filled Paige's glass. Paige took it, then got up, walked to the edge of the shack, peered out. Everything was dripping, and the crabs seemed to be relishing being all wet, were walking about each other, poking, pinching, ambling slowly about. Paige walked over to the cisterns, rapped one with a knuckle. The ping that came back made her think it was full of water.

"What is that?" Meg asked.

"Water collectors," Paige said. "Cisterns. They catch the rain, like John said, for drinking water."

Paige had never drunk rainwater before. She walked around the cistern and found a spigot, turned the knob. The thing fought a little before finally giving, and water poured out. She leaned over and took a sip of it, then turned off the spigot.

The water tasted like metal and sweetness. It was fairly warm, as everything on Palmer was warm. She wouldn't necessarily say it was refreshing, but it was at least fresh water.

She turned and looked back at the atoll, at the ribbon of jungle, at Meg close at hand in the shack. Paige thought she saw a bit of color in the distance, and a ripple in the water, but when she looked again, all she were ripples, nothing else.

The sun did not disappoint. It did come out, and she walked through the crabs to get back to the shack, if only for some sun protection.

"I should've brought my hat," she said. "Or some sunblock. Stupid me, I left it on the boat."

"Yes, you should always have a hat," Meg said. "The sun is positively deadly down here."

The older woman sipped her champagne, and Paige joined her, for there wasn't much else to do until the men returned. Paige wanted to see the sunset and get on the damned boat and leave Palmer Atoll far behind.

She pushed away some of the crabs, who had scuttled too close for comfort, and in so doing, dislodged a chunk of coral at the edge of the shack. She saw a little hole in the ground, and inside that hole, a Zip-Loc bag.

"Look," Paige said. "Buried treasure!"

She dug out the bag, and inside the dusty thing was a notebook. Meg looked on as Paige unsealed the bag, fished out the notebook. It was green, with spiral bindings.

Opening it, she saw that it was a journal. She thumbed through it and saw that the whole thing had been filled up with scrawled handwriting, barely legible. Black ink. There were sketches of crabs and seashells, competently rendered. And then a long, black tentacled thing from the water, grabbing a little man. Paige gasped, almost dropping the notebook.

"What does it say?" Meg asked. "Don't keep me in the dark, Darling."

Paige turned the notebook to face Meg, let her see the picture. The entry for August 15, 2012 said: "Kraken took Ronnie at dawn. Sun in our faces, couldn't see it. Too late. Ron's gone. I'm the only one left. I'm going to the treehouse. Fuck it."

"Whatever is a kraken?" Meg said.

"It's that thing," Paige said, holding the notebook steady so she could look at it in detail. Meg leaned in and looked closely at it, her eyes shaded behind her Jackie O sunglasses. "We need to leave."

Meg frowned, glanced over her shoulder at the lagoon, raked the jungle with her gaze, then looked back at the notebook. Paige could see the shadowed doubt in her eyes, the uncertainty.

"It's the same thing," Paige said. "What I saw."

Paige turned the notebook back to herself, sat down on the blanket beneath the shack, paged through it. The writer's name was Seth Parker. He was part of a three-person team from the Nature Preservancy, scouting out Palmer Atoll for acquisition and conservation. Seth Parker, Ron Wilson, and Angela Brewer.

She paged through it, noted the entries, read them to Meg. He'd been the one to pile up the cigarette lighters and other trash near the shack.

"'No sign of Angie; Ronnie doesn't know where she is. We combed Palmer for her, but no sign. *The Shady Lady* is still here, so we know she didn't sail off. We looked around for blood, for sharks, for anything. No sign. She's just gone.'"

Paige glanced at Meg, whose expression was masked by her thick frames, although her mouth was set in a stern, matronly line.

"'The radio's on the boat,'" Seth wrote. "'We're going to place a distress call. It's all we can do.'"

The next day was when Ronnie was taken by the thing. Then Seth went into the jungle, climbed a palm tree.

"'It's tall enough, I think,'" he wrote. "'I can't stay up here forever, but I think it can't reach me up here. Christ. The *Lady's* just 100 meters away. That's it. 100 meters. I swam that in college. I could make it. Or, I could wait it out.'"

Most of the journal from that point on was Seth waiting. And waiting. And waiting. And watching the kraken, writing about it.

"'It watches me,'" Seth wrote. "'I know it does. I can see it. Eyes like a goat's, those bizarre eyes. It watches me. The *Lady* dangling, like a prize. Floating. It knows.'"

Paige glanced at *Affinity*, licked her lips. Nearby, crabs crept toward the edge of the shack, claws probing the edge of Meg's blanket.

"'It lives in the lagoon,'" he said. "'That's its home. Somedays, safe in my treehouse, I can see it swimming. Beautiful and green-black. Horrible thing, but with monstrous grace. Using the *Lady* as a gauge, I think the kraken is at least one hundred feet long. Fucking huge. It glides through the water like a specter. Yesterday, it ate a shark that slipped into the lagoon. The shark just slid through the channel, and the thing snatched it up, throttled it. Didn't see what type; didn't matter. The kraken made short work of it—just thrashing and splashing and down it went with its prize. And I thought for a minute that maybe, just maybe I could swim for the *Lady* while the thing was busy tearing apart the shark. But then I thought that if something with many hundreds of millions of years of evolution behind it couldn't beat the kraken, what chance could I have? I just watched, rooted in place. I couldn't move.'"

"Sebastian?" Meg called, toward the jungle. "Sebastian? John?"

Storms hit Palmer for a long while, as Seth noted, the ink sometimes running on the pages. He had to get out of his tree perch, fearful of lightning striking him, went back to the shack for shelter.

"'Waves are washing over the atoll,'" Seth wrote. "'The *Lady's* rocking on her mooring, and everything's soaked. I've got no place to go. The waves are deafening. I'm tying myself to the shack. I couldn't stay up in the treehouse, get flung like I was in a catapult. Into the many loving arms of the kraken. I tied a bowline to my waist and said a prayer to King Neptune, to ride out the storm. Nobody's coming. There's just me. I'm going to seal this journal up in a baggie and bury it, hope somebody finds it. Get the hell out of here, whoever you are. The kraken is watching you. It can see you, wherever you go. It's smart. I'm going to take the kayak tomorrow. I can make it. I know I can.'"

Paige glanced at the kayak near the piled debris, while Meg called across the lagoon, her eyes on the jungle. That last entry was August 23, 2012.

"John? Sebastian?" she said.

"He didn't make it," Paige said. "He never got to his kayak."

"Sebastian?" Meg yelled, while Paige looked around for signs of struggle. For signs of anything. All she saw were crabs and jagged sand. The entry had been from a month before. That horrified her, the idea that poor Seth Parker was meeting his end only a month ago. That while she and John were having fun in Hawaii with the Trumbos, Seth Parker was fighting that monstrosity by himself, without another soul around to help him. People were so helpless when they were alone; people needed other people.

A crab shuffled near her foot, and Paige stepped away from it with a squawk. Those claws looked like they could nip her toes off with ease. She didn't want anything to do with them.

Sebastian came out of the jungle, to Meg's obvious relief. He looked disheveled, as what jungle that was there was thick, almost impassable.

"Sebastian!" Meg said. "We have to get out of here. We have to get to *Affinity*. There's something terrible in the water."

The older man looked at Meg quizzically, then over his shoulder. "Have you seen John?" he called, hands to his mouth.

"No," Meg said. "It's just been Paige and me. And that thing, we think."

Paige's eyes went to the jungle, her skin going cold, despite the oppressive humidity and heat of Palmer Atoll. John was nowhere to be seen.

"What happened?" Paige asked, as Sebastian got up to them. He grabbed for the champagne and drank it down, from the bottle.

"It was terribly thick in there," Sebastian said. "Although the water lapped close to our feet the whole time. We followed it along the curve of the atoll, but it was impossibly thick, for such a narrow little copse of trees. I've never seen anything like it. John and I got separated, and that was that. I thought he'd gotten ahead of me."

"No," Paige said. "We didn't see him. I think the kraken got him."

"Kraken?" Sebastian asked, his forehead wrinkling. Paige held open the journal, showed him some of the sketches. He looked them over, shook his head. "There's no such thing as a kraken. No octopus could get so big."

"Then it's a squid," Paige said. "I saw what I saw. A long tentacle, just like that."

"John!" Meg called. "John, honey, we're going to the boat. We don't want to leave you behind, Darling."

Sebastian handed the notebook to Paige, then turned back to the jungle.

"John," he yelled, cupping his hands to his mouth. "John, come out of there!"

Paige looked to the jungle, half-expected, half-hoping that John would emerge. How could the kraken snatch a man out of there? How could it even reach? She imagined a tentacle, like a great black snake, searching, and John, affable in his ignorance, walking through the jungle, a great adventurer in his own mind, stepping over exposed roots, wondering at little crabs sheltering in the shallows, hiding not from him, but from that thing, and John not even seeing the thing coming, snatching him up, catching him around his head, great suckers fixing fast to his face, impossibly strong, wrenching him upward, another tentacle wrapping around his chest, compressing him, forcing him down into the water, toward a snapping beak. Uncomprehending, to his death and dismemberment, warm ocean water filling his lungs while his struggles were restrained by cold embrace. Paige gasped.

"John," she cried. "Please, John."

"John!" Meg yelled. The three of them called out to him, loud as they were able to. And they waited between calls, waiting for something. But there was only the sound of the crashing waves, and the creak of the trees in the wind.

"There's no way some uppity mollusk snatched away your John," Sebastian said. "I don't even believe it. He's just having a bit of fun with us."

"But what about this?" Paige said, brandishing the notebook.

Sebastian looked at it with contempt. "The poor man went off his nut out here, all alone. He probably killed his shipmates and wrote some malarial memorandum for posterity, before throwing himself into the ocean. There are plenty of examples of that kind of madness taking someone. It's hard to know whether the ocean draws them, or compels them."

Paige wondered if the number one of the atoll's sign was for the kraken, and not for poor Seth Parker at all. She realized that the spraypainted warning could have been a sloppily-rendered octopus, what she thought had been the beard could have been its tentacles. She imagined Seth spraypainting it, desperately afraid of being caught by the thing as he did it.

"John!" Meg called. "John!"

Paige looked back, hoping he'd emerge from the jungle, but he didn't.

"John!" Sebastian yelled, then turned to the women, gesturing with the champagne bottle. "We can walk over there, see where he's gone to. Maybe he fell or something."

"That thing got him," Paige said.

"Nonsense," Sebastian said. "He's just on the far side of the lagoon."

"Sebastian," Meg said. "Take us to the *Affinity*. Right this instant."

Sebastian looked at his wife, then at Paige, a hint of incredulity on his tanned, weathered face. "Meg, let's suppose there is this beastie in the water, just the way Paige saw it. Do you think *Affinity* will be able to protect us from it?"

"There's a radio," Paige said. "We can call for help."

Sebastian conceded that point. "Fair enough, although I cannot imagine making that kind of a call on the radio. And we still have to find your John."

"John's gone," Paige said. She didn't know if for sure, but she felt it. There was simply no place for him to go on the atoll.

"We don't know that," Sebastian said. "But I'll get you two to the *Affinity* while I try to find John, if that makes you feel better."

Paige pointed at the dinghy, which had slipped from its moorings. Sebastian followed her gaze.

"That's certainly annoying," he said, striding after it, splashing up to his ankles to reach the dinghy. He reached for the towline with one hand, while holding the champagne bottle in the other.

All at once, the water exploded in a spray of tentacles, four of which grabbed Sebastian. Four tentacles wrapped around his arms, hoisting him aloft. The suckers were an ivory hue, had latched onto Sebastian's flesh as the glistening green-black tentacles coiled around him. He dropped the champagne bottle, managed a single scream, before being yanked underwater.

It happened so quickly that Paige and Meg didn't even have a chance to react to it—they started screaming after Sebastian had already vanished underwater.

The dinghy floated away from shore, like nothing had happened.

"Oh my God," Meg said. "Sebastian."

Paige watched for any sign of Sebastian, but there was nothing, just some fist-sized bubbles that broke the surface of the lagoon, and his Titan Electric Boat cap turning in a circle for a few moments, before it became soaked and sank.

"It grabbed him," Meg said, shaking, dropping to her knees.

Paige looked at the champagne bottle, sitting on the shore, spilling what was left of its contents into the sand. Beyond it, the dinghy, turning gently in the lagoon. And beyond that, the *Affinity*.

"We're going to die," Meg said.

TWO

MEG sobbed in her hands, sunglasses perched atop her head, while Paige looked around them, tried to figure out what to do. They just needed to get to *Affinity*, to get to the radio. Not that she knew how to work the radio, but she thought it'd not be impossible to operate.

"We have to get to the boat," Paige said.

Meg looked at her like she was insane. "That thing is out there, Paige. I'm not going anywhere near the water."

Paige sighed, gesturing around them. "Everywhere is near the water."

There was no sign of the kraken, but Paige knew it was there, somewhere. Meg was panicking, talking to herself, cursing.

"Meg," Paige said. "We have to keep our heads about this. Can you pilot the *Affinity*?"

"Yes," Meg said. "I've piloted boats, yes. This one is effectively a motorboat, so, yes. It might be tricky navigating through the lagoon, but otherwise, yes, yes, yes."

"Good," Paige said. "You may not have to. We just need to get to the boat, and to the radio. Call for help."

"Nobody might hear us," Meg said. "We're far away from everything."

"We can radio for help, and then pilot the boat out of the lagoon if we had to," Paige said. "Or we could just hide down inside it, wait to see if anybody came."

Some of the crabs had crept into the shelter, poking around, looking for things to steal.

"I don't see how we'll be able to reach the boat," Meg said. "Not with that thing swimming around."

Paige went to the edge of the lagoon, peering into the dark blue water. There was no sign of the thing. Then she thought about what she knew of cephalopods. They were supposed to be smart. She remembered something about that; they were capable of problem-solving.

Her problem was getting to *Affinity*, which meant getting the dinghy, which the kraken had really set up as a kind of trap, by pulling the dinghy away from the shore a bit.

"We could wait to see if the dinghy washes ashore," Paige said. "It's pretty calm in the lagoon, but there's still the wind blowing."

"That means just staying here?" Meg said. "Marooned?"

"Or I could try to swim for it," Paige said.

"No," Meg said. "No no no."

"There's also the kayak," Paige said. "I could use that to reach the *Affinity*."

Meg's tear-stained eyes turned to the kayak, almost forgotten amid the stacks of debris. She looked at it, looked at Paige, shook her head.

"It'll come for you," Meg said. "It'll take you like it took John and Sebastian."

Paige was getting impatient with Meg's endless naysaying. Both of them had lost their loved ones to this thing. Yes, perhaps Meg's was more traumatic because she'd actually seen it, but Paige's main concern was not suffering the same fate as the men had.

"Okay, Meg," Paige said. "What do you suggest?"

Meg sniffled, fought for composure. "I don't know. We wait, I suppose. Somebody else is bound to come to this atoll eventually."

Paige didn't relish the idea of just waiting here. Especially since it appeared that the thing could reach them at the shelter, judging from Seth's journal entries. He'd talked about the treehouse, one of the trees in the grove.

"Meg, I've got an idea," Paige said. "You can go into the grove across the lagoon, climb one of the trees over there. The one Seth called 'the treehouse.' Then you can keep an eye out for the kraken in the lagoon, while I kayak over to the *Affinity*."

Meg didn't like that idea that much, either, although she didn't say anything.

"We'll walk over there together," Paige said. "Try to find the tree."

Meg nodded, let Paige lead her along the edge of the atoll, toward the grove of trees. Paige watched the tides, was unsure what would happen with those, whether this area would be underwater during high tide. She'd never been on such a tiny spit of land before, had never felt so utterly at the mercy of the ocean. The contrast was striking—to their left, the inky calm of the lagoon; to their right, the surging waves of the Pacific Ocean, eating away at the atoll. There had been enough coral built up around the rim of the atoll to act as a bit of a buffer for the waves, but they crashed there just the same, the inexorable erosion that would inevitably claim Palmer Atoll.

They reached the stand of palms, the remnants of jungle that resided here. There were crabs aplenty in this place, and bugs, too, buzzing at them.

Paige looked around, saw a makeshift wooden treehouse up on one of the palms. She wondered if Seth had constructed that himself. She pointed, and Meg followed her gaze. Here, in the shelter of the palms, there was some measure of seeming security, although Paige had to remind herself that John had been taken here.

"How on Earth am I supposed to climb that?" Meg asked, gazing upward. There didn't seem to be any evident way up the tree.

"I don't know," Paige said. She wondered how Seth had done it. He was a young man and, most likely, had probably muscled his way up the trunk somehow. Paige doubted Meg had that in her.

From here, slightly elevated from the lower area at the far side of the lagoon, there was something of a view. But it would be better up in the treehouse—they'd be able to see more. Paige looked around, tried to find something they could use to get Meg up there.

"Is that thing a monster or an animal?" Meg asked.

"What do you mean?" Paige asked.

"A monster is something that is out to get us," Meg said. "An animal, I don't know—maybe it will get bored and leave us alone."

"It's both," Paige said.

Meg picked up a coconut and lobbed it into the lagoon. It landed with a splash, some distance away.

Paige winced, not wanting them to announce their position to the thing. But the splash brought it up. They could see it, this great, dark mass that rose from the depths of the lagoon. It had been there in seconds.

They could see its eyes, as big around as grapefruits, and yellow like that, with irises like bars. It studied the coconut, wrapping one of its great tentacles around the thing. The kraken was massive, looked like a great green slick just beneath the water.

"Meg," Paige said. "That's it. You can distract it over here. Keep throwing coconuts or stones to it. Keep it busy here, while I run back and get to the kayak, and reach *Affinity*."

She could see Meg processing it, thinking about her idea, and liking it. Hope had reappeared on her face. She hugged Paige.

"That's a great idea," Meg said.

The kraken lobbed the coconut back onshore with a hurl of its tentacle. The coconut landed with a thump.

Meg, emboldened, grabbed another one, tossed it out, far to the right of them. The great octopus pursued it, seized the coconut, studied it with its suckers.

Not wanting to waste any time, Paige ran back the way they had come, rushing to get to the shack. She'd slide that kayak into the water and row to the *Affinity*, hoping that Meg's distraction was enough.

The kraken lobbed the coconut back, and Meg called to it, this time throwing two coconuts at the same time. It was an absurd image, Meg and this monster octopus, playing catch.

Paige couldn't pause to reflect on it, however. She carefully but quickly shoved the kayak into the water, this clear plastic thing, which gave her an all-too-incredible view of the lagoon, made her uncomfortably aware of herself in the water. Then she paddled in the kayak, moving in clear, confident strokes toward the ketch.

From this position, she'd put the *Affinity* between herself and the kraken, hoping that it would screen her movements. She had kayaked enough times in Portland, and understood the nature of the rowing rhythm she needed to make good time.

She could hear Meg calling out, but over the noise of the waves beyond the atoll, could not hear what she was saying.

Paige had halved the distance to the *Affinity*, just kept pumping, her illness forgotten. There was only the single-minded determination to reach the boat.

Meg was screaming something, and Paige didn't have to guess what it was, as she saw the kraken slip noiselessly beneath her, perfectly visible through the clear kayak, which acted like a lens in the water. The sight of the thing so close, just a few feet below her, watching with its great eyes, studying her, tentacles trailing out behind it. It made Paige want to scream, but she refused to lose her focus.

The thing looked like malevolence incarnate, lurking below her, watching her row for the *Affinity*. Why didn't it strike? It changed its color, a marvelous transformation like a chameleon, going from that hideously smooth green-black to a lumpy, dusky red.

Then it swam up, pressing itself against the bottom of the kayak—all at once, the view vanished, became a bloom of suckers that stuck to the kayak, white and writhing, the size of teacups. In the heart of the sea of suckers, a great, blue-black beak, like a parrot's, as big as a man's head. The beak scraped at the kayak, gave it an exploratory nibble that scratched the plastic.

The drag on the kayak was profound. The weight of the thing had brought Paige to a halt. She could not move. Around her, the tentacles of the kraken splashed in the water. The thing swam, taking her away from the ketch, moving her into the depths of the lagoon, in full view of Meg, who was screaming.

Paige was screaming, too, seeing that great big beak, just centimeters from her thigh. She was not going to be food for this thing.

She raised her oar and whacked at one of the tentacles, struck at it, but the oar was a clumsy weapon, merely slapped against the thing's hide.

Then it yanked the oar from her hands with another of its tentacles, and tossed it at Meg, an almost offhand motion, a careless lob that sent the thing spinning end over end.

Then, all at once, it released Paige, swam down into the depths of the lagoon. Paige could see it down there, watching her.

"Why did it spare you?" Meg asked, her voice quavering.

"I think it's playing with its food," Paige said, wanting to cry. There was no way she'd be able to swim for the *Affinity* before that thing caught her.

It just sat there in the depths, nowhere near the bottom, and watched her. It wanted to see what she was going to do.

"It's not fair," Meg said.

Paige furtively took her hands to either side of the kayak and began gently paddling, steering herself toward the ketch, and then moving toward it with careful splashes of her hands, her eyes beneath her, on the kraken.

The thing just watched. It had changed its color again, was now a muddy green-brown, but its bright yellow eyes were fixed on her.

Paige paddled toward the ketch, refused to let herself be sport for the monstrous thing in the water. She glanced at Meg, who was silent, watching.

There was something else, too—the sun was no longer so high in the sky. The sun would set soon, and if it was bad dealing with the thing by daylight, nighttime would be far worse. Paige resolved that, one way or another, she would not still be floating in the lagoon come nightfall.

The kraken had crept back up while she was thinking, and was, again, just below her, looking up at her through the clear-bottomed kayak with its great yellow eyes.

Paige stopped her paddling with her hands, instinctively drew herself in, choked back a scream. The octopus had spread itself out, and looked to be at least 20 feet in diameter, like some great, horrible carpet that ended in tentacle fringe.

A lone tentacle snaked out of the water, slapped against the kayak, and pulled it away from the *Affinity*.

"Why isn't it eating you?" Meg cried.

"It ate John and Sebastian," Paige said. "It's not hungry right now."

She didn't know this for sure, but felt it was about as good an answer as any. Why wouldn't a monstrous octopus want to play? Who knew how many times this thing had played this kind of game with visitors to the atoll? If it had seen this played out enough times, it likely understood that the tiny people seemed to really want to get to their big floating shelters.

Paige wondered how old the kraken was, how long it had lived at this place, whether it migrated, whether it was alone, or whether there were others, whether it was male or female.

It slid the kayak across the lagoon with a shove of its tentacles, and Paige saw the *Affinity* slip far away from her as she went back into the deep section.

"What are we going to do?" Meg asked, crying again.

Paige's mind raced as she tried to think of something. The kayak was a good idea, but it wasn't working for her right now.

She paddled toward the dinghy, taking a long route around the *Affinity*, glanced down to see what the kraken was doing. It had retreated again to the depths, but was watching, though.

Paige reached the dinghy, and grabbed the towline, tied it to the kayak, and then paddled for the shore, her eyes on the octopus, which simply watched.

Did octopuses sleep? Paige did not know.

She got the dinghy and the kayak ashore, jumped out and dragged the kayak to the shack, tied it to one of the support poles of the shelter.

Then she dragged the dinghy to the shelter, straining her arms, but fueled by adrenaline, seeing the octopus again close to the surface, silently watching her.

Paige retreated to the supposed safety of the shack, collapsed there, gasping. She was exhausted, both physically and mentally.

She took out Seth's journal, added an entry of her own.

SEPTEMBER 20, 2012

If you're reading this, you're on this atoll, and maybe you've seen it, or maybe you just discovered Mr. Parker's journal. Get off Palmer Atoll. The creature he describes is real. I'm one of two survivors of the Affinity—*it already took John Marsden and Sebastian Trumbo.*

Meg Trumbo and I (Paige Wilkins), are trapped on the shore. This is our first day here, and the thing attacked immediately. It took John, although nobody saw it happen. The atoll is tiny, and he disappeared. He's missing and presumed dead.

We saw it take Sebastian. It just grabbed him with its tentacles and yanked him underwater, killing and no doubt eating him, although I didn't see blood in the water, it could be because it dragged him down to its lair in the depths of the lagoon.

Meg and I made several attempts to reach the Affinity, *but it thwarted them. In fact, it played a little game with me—the thing is intelligent, to be sure—it kept letting me paddle toward our boat, but would pull me away from it when I neared it.*

I think it wasn't hungry at the time, which led it to toy with me. It seems to understand that we're not going anywhere if we can't reach our boat.

> *Which makes me wonder—what happened to the* Shady Lady? *Did the thing sink it? I was so preoccupied with trying to stay alive, that I admit that I didn't look for it in the lagoon.*
>
> *It will be sunset, soon. This may be our last night alive. I'm not sure. If we survive the morning, I'll try to see if there are shipwrecks in the depths of the lagoon. If it can't sink the* Affinity, *that offers us at least the hope that someone, somewhere, may be able to rescue us. Or maybe the kraken is smart enough to take the ship away from the shelter of the lagoon. I don't know. Time will tell. All I know is that right now, I'm alive, which isn't saying much.*

Meg had turned up, carrying the kayak oar like it was a weapon, her eyes wild.

"It was playing with you," Meg said. "Like you were a toy. I saw everything."

"Yes," Paige said, putting the journal back into the baggie, sealing it up, returning it to its hiding place.

"It'll be sunset, soon," Meg said. "Our lovely Pacific sunset, here, you and me, and that thing."

"Yes," Paige said. "We have to make another attempt for the *Affinity* in the morning. Forget the radio: we should activate the EPIRB."

All sea vessels carried EPIRBs, which were emergency radio distress beacons. Activating that would send a signal that would draw rescuers. She wasn't sure if the Coast Guard even had jurisdiction in these remote waters, but assumed there'd be some kind of response.

Meg sat down, set the oar across her lap, after using it to shoo away some of the crabs, which were milling about.

"It has these crabs here," Meg said. "It has an ocean teeming with fish—why does it even eat us?"

"For sport?" Paige said. "I don't know. Maybe it got into the habit, became a maneater. Maybe this is its idea of fun."

"That's evil," Meg said.

Something else occurred to Paige as she sat, watching darkness slowly come to the east, saw the sun get low in the west. A night here would be frightening, with only the crash of the waves and the absolute darkness around them, and that kraken, lurking out there somewhere.

At any rate, what she understood was that, as mighty and large as that octopus was, there were still two of them to one of it. So, it could not be in two places at once. That meant that if one of them distracted it properly, the other should be able to reach the *Affinity* and activate the EPIRB.

Looking at Meg seated across from her, Paige wondered how she'd be able to pitch that plan to her. It looked like Meg was hanging on by her manicured fingernails at this point.

"I can't imagine another day here," Meg said.

"You're assuming we survive until morning," Paige said.

"A big IF," Meg said, laughing bitterly, giving another of the coconut crabs a shove with the oar.

"We can both go in the water," Paige said. "One of us as bait for the kraken, the other attempting to reach the *Affinity*."

"Oh, I don't like that plan one little bit," Meg said.

"It's the only idea I have left at the moment," Paige said. "It can't be in two places at once. I don't care how big or fast it is. The lagoon is bigger than that thing is. So, I'll go into the water in the kayak, will paddle across the way, as far as I can go, hoping that the thing will come up and be occupied with me. And while that's happening, you take the dinghy and motor over to the *Affinity*. You board, you activate the EPIRB, call on the radio, too, and we get help to come."

Meg quietly considered it, perhaps happy that she wasn't the one who was going to be the bait.

"And what happens to you?" Meg asked.

"I'll paddle for the far shore of the lagoon, hope that I can make it," Paige said. "I'm only a distraction. The point is, with two of us, we can do this. We just have to work together."

Meg whacked another of the coconut crabs with the oar, sending the thing lumbering away.

"If we make it through to morning, I'll at least consider it," Meg said.

They watched the sunset together, saw the flash of green as the sun went beneath the waves, and saw themselves dropped into the darkest night either of them had ever known, with only the endless crash of surf and the whistle of wind to break the silence that enfolded them.

THREE

SLEEP came, despite their circumstances. Paige dreamed of the kraken, worshipped by islanders, tribesmen, who fed it criminals bound to rafts, while the islanders danced on the shore, beating drums to awaken the thing, saw the doomed soul gaze in horror as the great octopus swam up and wrapped the man in its tentacles and dragged him down. The islanders wore paint on their faces, black ink, and flailed their arms in a ghoulish, worshipful parody of the kraken.

Paige woke with a start, looking around them, feeling her way in the dark. Meg was there beside her, curled up in a ball. Some coconut crabs were creeping around, poking and prodding with their great claws.

Paige's stomach growled. They'd need to eat something in the morning.

Around her, it was so incredibly dark. She gazed skyward, saw the stars like she had never seen them before, on the purest, blackest canvas overhead. It was dazzling, and, even in these dreadful circumstances, she was struck by the ungodly beauty of those uncaring stars.

She sniffed the air, the warm sea air. This place was so close to the Equator, it was unbelievably hot. She went to the cistern and took a drink of water from the spigot, then poured some into that hanging tin cup, rinsed the salt spray from it. Paige cleaned out the cup, put it under the spigot and drank the rainwater, drank three cups of it, grateful that the cistern was even here. If it had not been, they would be halfway dead by now in this tropical heat.

Paige thought about the octopus. In Hawaii, their mythology held that the octopus was the only survivor of a previous, alien world that had been destroyed before the time of man. She could see that, could imagining them seeing them that way. They were alien things. She remembered a boyfriend in her youth who was a fan of Cthulhu, the octopus-faced creation of H.P. Lovecraft, who had a bunch of Cthulhu-related merchandise at his place. Robby Kramer. He'd been studying to be an accountant in college. She wondered if he'd become one, imagined him packing away all of his Cthulhu toys as he'd become a responsible adult. Or maybe he'd created his own shrine to it, used the money he made at his job to make his childhood collection into some full-blown adult obsession. She smiled to herself. Robby Kramer would be beside himself with envy at Paige's current predicament.

She drank another ladle of water, carefully closed the spigot to the cistern, and hung the tin cup again.

Then she saw that the dinghy and the kayak were gone.

Paige gasped aloud, ran to where she had moored them. She saw that the rope had been snapped, and she cursed.

In the darkness of a moonless night, she could not see the boats. The thing had snuck up when they were sleeping, had pulled the boats free. More of its sport, she imagined. It knew this game.

Paige doubted that Meg would be willing to enter into the water on her own, to swim for it. Paige doubted she'd do that, herself. It would be a variant of their earlier attempt, with one person as the distraction, and the other making their way for the boat.

It galled Paige that she'd invariably be the one who assumed all the risk—that Meg, even with their lives in the balance, wouldn't commit to taking that kind of chance. No doubt Meg's whole life had been one of some form of risk-aversion. Maybe she'd never encountered anything like that before, having sheltered under Sebastian's coattails for however many years they had been together. Paige had forgotten to ask.

Paige didn't know what time it was, could not venture a guess in the dark, but saw phosphorescence in the water, and was, despite her fear and frustration, fascinated by it. There were swirling patterns of greenish hue, radiant and glowing, moving this way and that.

She followed the patterns with her eyes, only to realize that they flowed along eight points, terminating in a large and bulbous center. It was the kraken, glowing there in the dark, covered with a phosphorescent slime, just out of reach, in the water, watching her.

Paige yelped, backed away, tripping over a crab, which she picked up and threw into the water at the octopus.

The crab splashed clumsily, was swiftly wrapped in tentacles, drawn below the surface. Paige watched the glowing tentacles slither and slide as the kraken consumed the coconut crab. She could not see the entire scene, could only make out the glowing movements.

She went to the far side of the shelter, putting herself as far from the lagoon as she could go, on the windward side, and laid back down, tried to get more sleep, while her mind worked and she thought about what they could possibly do. She'd almost wanted to wake up Meg, to tell her about their dire situation, but didn't want to put up with Meg's wailing.

Paige just rolled on her back, only half-covered by the tin roof of the shelter, and gazed up at the stars.

Turns out, she was awakened by Meg's wailing, anyway, as Meg had apparently discovered that the boats had been moved.

"They're gone," Meg said. "Paige, wake up. They're gone."

Paige jolted awake, reflexively swinging with her arms. She'd been dreaming about the kraken again, wrapping her in its soft, insistent tentacles, dragging her into the depths, far from light and life, its great beak pressed against her face, cold and horrible.

Paige looked, saw the dinghy and the kayak were in the center of the lagoon, a few hundred feet from the *Affinity*.

"So much for your grand plan," Meg said. "It seems that the octopus has other things in mind for us."

Meg began to cry, while Paige looked around them. "We have to eat something. I suggest crab."

"Can we eat them? Are they safe?"

"I don't know," Paige said. "Only one way to find out."

She wasn't going to let Meg just sob through their morning. "Pick up any driftwood you see, Meg. Gather it up, bring it here."

"Beg pardon?" Meg asked.

"I'm going to try to get a fire going," Paige said. "Maybe we can cook some crab with it. Maybe we can use it to send a column of smoke to the sky, draw in somebody."

Meg snuffled, considered it. "Okay, I'll gather wood."

"Please be careful," Paige said.

Paige was grateful that she at least did that, and then went about going through the pile of cigarette lighters, trying to find one that still worked. One by one, Paige tested them, saw which ones had any movement left on the wheels, which ones could spark, which ones could flame. As she sorted, she was amazed and appalled at the amount of litter there was, how people could be so sloppy and slovenly, as careless to just dump things like this into the beautiful ocean. The beautiful ocean that housed monstrosities like the kraken, she had to remind herself.

She sorted through hundreds of lighters, and managed to find a dozen that still worked. The working ones she put in her pockets, not trusting to leave them out where the crabs or perhaps the kraken could reach them.

Then she had an idea, took some of the netting and the other plastic, and she dragged that away from the other piles, and then made a pile of its own. Plastic would burn in a toxic, smoky haze. If she could create a smoke line that went up into the sky, that might catch someone's attention.

At this point, Paige was prepared to do any number of things.

So, she made her pile of netting, banking it carefully, since she didn't want to set the entire atoll ablaze, obviously, and then she cracked some of the nonworking lighters, spilled their isobutane fuel onto the plastic pile, and tossed the empty cases on the pile afterward.

Then she carefully took one of the functional lighters and she struck it, was gratified to see the fire whoosh to life, fueled by the isobutane, and immediately set upon the plastic, sending curls of acrid smoke up into the sky.

The winds were strong, were blowing the smoke eastward, but at least it was going up.

Paige was pleased with herself, pocketed the lighter and began grabbing armloads of netting and put it on the plastic blaze, watching how quickly the fire consumed the plastic, watching the smoke go skyward.

She was careful not to breathe it, not wanting to give herself an asthma attack. She kept feeding the fire until the plastic bottles and most of the netting were all used up, until the plastic blaze was practically a bonfire, watched the smoke line go ever higher.

"Meg," Paige called. "Look!"

But there was no Meg. Paige looked across the atoll, toward the grove, where Meg had gone, and didn't see her.

Her satisfaction at her makeshift signal fire curdled within her.

No.

She ran from the shelter area, past the whooshing fire, along the lip of the lagoon, calling out Meg's name as she went. There was no sign of her.

"No no no no," Paige said, almost reflexively. She searched, her eyes wild, saw a bundle of driftwood on the ground, saw one of Meg's sandals, saw her big sunglasses in the grass. Of course, there was no Meg.

Her eyes dragged to the lagoon, where the kraken lurked somewhere. Meg's other sandal floated in the water, moving in a counterclockwise circle.

"You bastard," Paige said. "You fucking bastard!"

She screamed, stomped her feet, actually grabbed the other sandal and lobbed it into the lagoon.

Then she collapsed and cried into her hands. It wasn't fair. Meg had probably just turned her back to the lagoon for a moment, didn't think that the thing might have been watching her, but, to Paige's eye, it was perfectly situated to see her here. She picked up Meg's sunglasses and put them on. Paige was going to fry on this island, without access to sunblock. She had to shelter.

She imagined Meg with her armload of driftwood, maybe even distracted by Paige's signal fire, her eyes on that, as the kraken shot a couple of its telephone pole-sized tentacles out at her, grabbing her, yanking her into the water before the poor woman could so much as scream.

The thing had technique. It knew how to hunt its atoll. This was very clear to Paige. Again, she wondered how long this monster had lived here, whether it had moved in, or whether it had always been here. She resolved to discover the history of Palmer Atoll when she got back to *Affinity*.

Not if; when. She watched the smoke travel messily upward, great gouts of it as the plastic was consumed. The plastic fire would not last for long, so she gathered up the driftwood that Meg had collected, mindful of the lagoon, and then walked back to the shelter, made another pile upwind of the plastic, built it around the hibachi, and then stuck one of the sticks into the gooey burning plastic, and got the driftwood branch to burn, and then stuffed that into the stack of wood, hoping it would take.

She grabbed some dead palm leaves and put those on the wood fire, too, hoping they would act as tinder. The wood burned fitfully, cracking and popping, but it did burn, and then Paige was occupied with growing that fire. She would need to make visits to the grove, grabbing more things that would burn, to keep that fire going.

Then she'd have to kill one of those great, big coconut crabs. She did not look forward to that, but she had no intention of starving on this island, either.

Having things to do, little tasks, kept her from giving in to despair. It bothered her that both John and Meg had vanished without so much as a sound, that a couple of human lives had been extinguished so arbitrarily. It could have been her. She could have been gathering the wood, and the octopus could have snagged her, instead.

No, she would have been more careful. That's what she told herself. She would have been very alert, watching for it. Meg had probably been distracted, hadn't maintained that necessary situational awareness to keep safe.

Paige gathered handfuls of dead palm leaves, a handful of fresh green ones, and a few more chunks of driftwood.

Or, maybe the monster let Paige set that signal fire, because it remembered, it knew that such fires drew more prey to it.

That thought actually stopped Paige a moment in her tracks, made her gaze into the lagoon, which was as dark and clear and opaque as ever. *Affinity* loomed, and the dinghy and the kayak did a little circular waltz in the center of the lagoon.

The thing could not be that smart, could it? Could it understand fire?

Paige would not believe that, assumed that it simply had not seen her working, had gone after Meg, who was the easier prey from a favorite hunting ground. The thing clearly liked the grove, so Paige resolved to be extra cautious around there.

She dumped the gathered fuel for the fire, watched the plastic blaze settle into a black, gooey scar to the side, and grabbed a dozen more plastic bottles, tossed those onto that fire, too, watched them curl and twist into blackened, burning nothingness.

It could have been Paige who had been taken. She'd gotten caught up in her little fire-building. One of those tentacles could have simply snatched her away, as it had the others.

She saw that the champagne bottle Sebastian had been carrying when he'd been taken was now gone. No doubt the thing had taken it for its collection, down at the bottom of the lagoon, part of its monstrous garden.

Paige imagined it in its garden, playing with the cracked skulls of hundreds of victims, arranging them, stacking them, delighting in their nice, round shape, the whiteness of the bone, far from the light, adding that nice, glass bottle of Dom Perignon to it, perhaps one of hundreds of bottles.

She shuddered. Then she took the last of the netting and unworked a tangle of it, until she had a kind of basket made, something she could hang over her shoulder. Then Paige collected coconuts, walking as far as she could along the atoll, filling the net-bag with them, getting a half-dozen of them in there.

Paige saw on the windward side of the atoll, saw the piles of litter washed up. Palmer had no end of litter on hand. She resolved to search it out the following morning, assuming she survived the night, to see if there was anything useful to be had, there. Even if it was just fuel for the fire, it would serve.

She looked around, saw the sky was full of roiling white clouds, felt her skin cooking in the tropical sun, made her way back to the shelter and dumped the coconuts.

Then she bashed one of the crabs to death with one of the coconuts, took the washtub and filled it with seawater, and set it atop the hibachi, hoped that the heat wouldn't melt the washtub. She tossed some of the green palm leaves into the fire. The green leaves threw off nice, white smoke that was more fragrant than the plastic fire, which was now burning itself out, so Paige grabbed a few more plastic bottles and tossed them onto it, just to keep it going.

Seth Parker would not have approved, she knew. The Nature Preservancy would be disappointed in this destruction and pollution of Palmer Atoll, and she sympathized. She didn't like it, either. But she needed someone to see her. She needed this desperately.

Paige knew that you were ideally supposed to throw a live crab into a boiling pot of water, but didn't relish the prospect of wrestling a giant hermit crab, probably losing a few fingers to its claws, only to either have the thing crawl out of the washtub or else watch it die as it boiled to death. Nature could be cruel, and human nature, no less cruel.

The water boiled, the crab cooked, and Paige's stomach growled. She tended both fires, kept them both going, and, when she saw the crab's shell turn color, used a driftwood branch to pry it out of the boiling washtub. She set the crab on a bed of green palm leaves, and let it cool.

She would remove the washtub from the fire once it had boiled off the water.

Paige then used a coconut to crack the crab's shell, carefully prying out the hot, delicious meat with her fingers. She gobbled it down, ate every bit of the crab she could reach, until she was stuffed.

Then, on a whim, she tossed the empty leavings into the lagoon, imagined it settling downward, onto the kraken. Another pile of trinkets for its aquatic garden.

Paige felt better, having eaten, and drank deep of the cistern, and, at least for the moment, was grateful to be alive. Careful to keep her eyes on the lagoon, she fished out Seth Parker's journal, made another entry.

SEPTEMBER 21, 2012

The kraken got Meg. I didn't see it happen. I had been busy creating a signal fire, using some of the plastic litter that was piled up here. The amount of debris washing ashore here is saddening and maddening. I'm going to the north shore of the atoll tomorrow, to root through the debris, and see if I can find anything useful in there.

Been busy today. I managed to salvage 20 working cigarette lighters out of this great pile of them that somebody—Seth? Somebody else?—had made. For all I know, it could have been another person like me, marooned on this island, trying to avoid the monster that waited in the water.

Affinity *is where she's been since we docked here. The octopus has not sunk it, so maybe it can't. I haven't figured out what I'm going to do, yet, how I'm going to get to the boat, but I will.*

Despite the loss of Meg, I have remained productive. I have made a cookfire out of driftwood and boiled a coconut crab upon it. It was delicious, heavenly to my empty stomach. And I gathered up a number of coconuts, which I'll either crack open myself, or else use as bait to draw in coconut crabs, have them open them, and then will kill and eat them and the coconut, as well. I know that sounds ruthless, but what else am I going to do?

I'm battling some rather serious sunburn, but, again, I am not going to travel the island at night. It's simply too risky.

The octopus is still out there, although it's been fairly quiet today. Maybe killing Meg provided it enough sport. I'm not sure. I will share my own insights into the monster in this journal, add to Mr. Parker's own observations.

It is most definitely an intelligent creature, however monstrous it may appear. Two of our party were taken near the grove, so if you are reading this, if you are stranded here as I have been, take care around there. I'm not sure why that area is so deadly. It could simply be that there is the appearance of safety there, in terms of elevation and the presence of trees, but I'd stress that in no place is the atoll higher than a bit over 5 feet—no place is actually safe, as I understand it. At least within the confines of the lagoon, I think any area can be reached by the creature. I'm not sure if it ventures out of the lagoon and travels around on the windward side of the island or not. It certainly could if it wanted to.

Anyway, beware the grove. There is a tempting shelter there, Parker's Perch, as I'm calling it. He seemed to scale it, and was apparently out of reach of the beast there. I may attempt it before nightfall, see what I can do, whether I can manage it. It beats spending another night at the shack, which is in full reach of the monster.

I hope to be able to write more tomorrow.

Paige closed the book, and again carefully stowed it, sealed it, placed it in its hiding place. She was grateful for it, to be honest, found some relief in speaking to posterity in that way, assuming something happened to her, which was entirely possible. Likely, even.

Taking another deep drink of water, Paige shut its spigot and then carefully drew the washtub out of the cookfire with a branch, set it on the ground.

The kraken tentacle snaked out of the water, making Paige yelp as she dodged it, seeing the thing search for her, dripping, shiny, and wet.

It landed on the washtub, and then recoiled as there was a hiss of steam as its wet limb touched the scalding hot metal.

The tentacle vanished back into the lagoon in a flash, and Paige laughed through gritted teeth, glad that the thing had hurt itself.

"Take that, Monster," she said.

Then she went toward the grove, headed for Parker's Perch, very careful to keep her eyes on the lagoon, to be sure that the thing didn't get the drop on her there. Then she got beneath the treehouse, and tried to figure out how Seth got up there, hoping it wasn't simply an exercise in manly muscle, because although she was fit, she was unsure if she were fit enough to scale a palm tree barehanded.

There was a cluster of palms near the treehouse, which itself looked to be placed between several other trees. Paige thought if she climbed one of the smaller trees like it was a pole, just inching her way up, that maybe this would let her reach the treehouse.

She did so, positioning herself so that she could keep an eye on the lagoon, and slowly scaled the tree this way, like a great inchworm. From here, in this fashion, she was able to do this, although she was uncomfortable, since she would be completely at the mercy of the kraken, if it saw her and chose to pluck her from the tree.

Paige scaled it, until she was level with the treehouse, which was really just some planking that had been nailed up here.

She extended a foot, reaching out for the thing, and was gratified that her foot found ready purchase on the wood. She listened for creaking, and didn't hear anything that alarmed her, and then she carefully stepped out onto the thing, letting out a sigh of relief when she'd reached it.

She squawked a moment later, seeing three coconut crabs sheltering in the thing. Cursing, Paige grabbed at them and evicted them from the treehouse, hurling them into the lagoon, one after another. She was not in a sharing mood, least of all with those 40-pound crabs. The octopus snagged the crabs, dragged them into the depths, wrapping its mantle around all three of them in one pass, its golden eyes unreadable as it sank, changing colors from green-black to brown to red as it dropped from sight for a moment. Paige hoped that maybe by feeding the thing, it would be less prone to just gobble her up when the opportunity presented itself. That was her hope, and there seemed to be plenty of crabs left on the atoll, at least for now.

Up here, she felt better, could get some perspective, could actually see around them. She could see her fading fires at the shelter, could see the smoke trails blowing eastward. Could see the boats in the lagoon, could see beyond the confines of Palmer Atoll, could see the churning indigo expanse of the Pacific Ocean, and the endless horizon, the mountains of clouds.

And, of course, in the dark of the lagoon, she could see the kraken had returned already, that great, big, horrible thing, looking up at her with its great eyes, just floating in the water, beneath the surface, like some malevolent star.

To be safe from it filled her with delight, despite everything that had happened.

"You can't get me here," Paige said, sticking her tongue out at it. She felt like she stood upon a rampart, taunting the besieging army below her.

The kraken did not respond, just watched. It had turned itself an inky blue, a beautiful hue that played well to its golden eyes.

Parker's Perch was a shelter, but was not a sanctuary. Paige resolved to spend her nights here, but would have to venture down for supplies from the shelter, had to travel that gauntlet. It was enough for now.

She watched the sun set from up there, watched another night fall on the island, saw the orange-red glow of her fading fires, saw the phosphorescence of the octopus in the lagoon, watched the green flash as the sun fell beneath the horizon, ending the day, saw the night sky rise, saw the quarter moon appear.

Paige watched these things until she fell asleep. She did not dare to dream.

—

FOUR

PAIGE awoke to have a coconut crab pinching her shoe. She started, sat up, and saw that it was morning. The crab was at the edge of the ledge, standing there with its legs splayed out, feelers moving, pincer prodding her foot.

She pried her shoe free of the thing, and then, in a fit of pique, grabbed the great crab and hurled it into the lagoon.

Paige watched the thing tumble and saw the kraken catch it before it hit the water, shooting a tentacle from the depths to grab it and take it underwater.

"Good morning to you, too," Paige said, grumbling. She was stiff and sore—not that the planking was any less comfortable than the ground she'd been sleeping on. It all sucked.

She looked around from her perch, disappointed that no ships had come. Maybe they had not seen the smoke from the island.

Paige had a bunch of bug bites to go with her sunburn, had to will herself not to scratch them.

The sky was cloudy, and it smelled like rain to her. She was hungry, and, taking another look around from the high perch, climbed down from there, mindful of the lagoon.

The atoll was like a giant letter G, she thought, with the open part representing the entrance to the lagoon. She was down at the lowest part of the G, and the shack was at the top of the bottom, facing across the entry point of the lagoon.

Today, after she fed, she'd walk the length of the atoll, just to see what, if anything, could be had, there.

She stomped back into her campsite, past the black scar of the melted plastic, and the ash of her cookfire, into the shelter. The crabs had gotten into her coconuts, and had opened a few of them.

Paige took advantage of that to drink down what coconut milk was left, and to bash the opened coconuts open wider, digging out the meat with her fingers. She looked around as she ate, chewing, thinking, planning, scheming.

Her eyes were drawn to something white, at the edge of the shelter. She jumped, seeing a pile of skulls. Human skulls, in a massive stack, all of them clean and white, all of them missing their lower jaws, all of them with a wedge-shaped gouge taken out of the skull.

"My God," Paige said, almost dropping the coconut meat.

She could not bear to see these things staring at her, or worse, that the octopus had arranged them this way for her to see them. Was it gloating at her? Attempting to communicate?

Paige got up and stomped over to the skulls, then picked one up, threw it back into the lagoon, watched it splash and sink. She'd never held a skull before, had acted without thinking, fueled by irritation and outrage.

"You won't scare me," Paige said. "You hear me, Monster? I'm not scared."

Then she lobbed each and every skull back into the lagoon, counting as she did so. She got to 315 when the last skull vanished from view.

She wondered if any of the skulls were those of her friends. If any of them were Seth Parker. Paige backed away from the edge of the lagoon, into the shelter, and sat down, choked down some more coconut meat, her appetite killed by the grim spectacle.

Paige fished out the journal, made an entry.

> SEPTEMBER 22, 2012
>
> Slept at Parker's Perch, unmolested during the night, except for a couple of those crabs, which seem to have no problem getting up there.
>
> The kraken left me a present in the morning: it had piled up skulls of its victims—I have no idea if it was all of them, but I threw them back into the lagoon, and the number counted 315. This thing appears to have taken at least 315 human lives.
>
> I don't know if it was showing off, or displaying these to frighten me, or whether it just wanted me to understand that this would be my fate. The monster is intelligent. I wish that I could communicate properly with it, although I don't think it would care. With 315 victims to its credit, what does that make me? Just another skull for its collection, it would seem.

It looks like rain, and I don't want this journal to get lost, so I'm stowing it again. My plan today, barring rain, is to travel the length of the atoll, see what's there, and what, if anything, I might salvage. From Parker's Perch, I can see that the atoll is roughly G-shaped, so there is a wide, windward expanse of that lengthy curve of the G to explore. Maybe there'll be something. I have to try.

Until next time,
Paige Wilkins

Paige didn't know why she signed that entry, mulling over that as she carefully sealed it up and placed it in its hiding place.

The rain came shortly thereafter, a great torrent that churned up the lagoon and set the ocean waves beyond it crashing and smashing. It was a full-blown storm, and Paige shivered beneath the tin roof of the shelter, all but deafened by the sound of the heavy rain upon it.

The kraken was invisible to her in the lagoon, because the sheets of rain that fell made it impossible to see.

All at once, a dangerous, desperate idea came to Paige. With this heavy rain falling, maybe she could risk swimming across the lagoon to reach the *Affinity*. It was perhaps possible that all the noise from the storm, all of the action on the lagoon, would conceal her.

She looked out into the dark lagoon, which was pummeled by the falling rain, and reconsidered it. For all she knew, the octopus was just under the surface, waiting for her.

Instead, she sat down in the center of the shelter, shivering, and ate coconut meat. Lightning crashed and thunder rumbled, and Paige watched this, saw *Affinity* move with the rolling waves, where even the lagoon was affected by the surge of the storm.

To be on this tiny atoll in a storm was almost as bad as facing the kraken, itself. Paige felt impossibly small in the face of it, watched the waves crash against the coral shallows, feared that something bigger might come along and smash her.

And, just as it had come, the storm passed, and the island was again quiet, dripping, the crabs scuttling around, and Paige on her feet, shivering in the momentary chill, watching the stormclouds blast eastward. The heat would return, but in the immediate wake of the storm, it was chilly.

She walked the length of the atoll, past the grove, along the windward lip of the place, seeing the great Pacific Ocean waves smashing against the reef, saw the piles of plastic litter accumulated there, bleached profusion of colors—red, yellow, orange, blue, green, white—festive, mercenary hues, the detritus from countless consumer marketing campaigns, tossed overboard. What the products even were could not be determined—now, they were only bottles and baskets and other sundry items. Paige would wade through them all, once the surf hopefully died down.

She kept going along the length of the atoll, could see the great curve of it, saw more palm tree groves, hanging onto their tiny bit of land for dear life, one of the palms at a roughly 30-degree angle. The crabs watched her as she passed. Nobody went out this way, as the palms grew thicker, here.

This portion of the atoll looked more menacing. Something about the thickness of the palms here made it so, and there was something else. Although the beach was broader here along the north side of it, for the G of the atoll was on its side, with the long curve of it facing north, there were also submerged shallows here, separating the land from itself. The ground was more treacherous, here, the footing, less certain.

Paige had reached the edge of the thickest part of the jungle, what she decided to call the Thicket, and saw that she'd have to splash through some shallows to reach the next point of land, reflected in a tangled thickness of trees.

She splashed through the shallows, then went to the next pile of land, which was even more densely packed with trees.

In her view, this was the proper place for a sanctuary. The lagoon was nearby, but there were more trees here. This place could offer more protection from the octopus, or at least appeared to.

There were lots of bugs here, though, and she was swatting at them almost constantly. Maybe that's what put people off of this area, plus, the anchorage was on the other side, closer to the shelter.

Paige tramped through the narrow strip of jungle, kept scanning around her, both the horizon and also the lagoon. She saw a container ship at great distance, almost over the horizon, and felt a surge of sorrow and longing, seeing that big vessel.

There was no way she'd be able to get them to see her, not at this place. And seeing the world going on its way while she was stuck here, it actually served to almost weaken her resolve, if only for a moment. When *Affinity* had not reported in at her appointed time, maybe, just maybe the folks at Titan Electric Boat would send someone. Assuming it was even listed as overdue. There was no way of knowing what Sebastian and John had arranged ahead of the trip. Since it was a shakedown cruise, maybe they had prepared for the possibility of mishap or equipment failure, and had something in place. That helped Paige get herself composed again.

It wasn't so terrible, was it? Right now, she had food, she had water. She could survive here as long as the thing didn't get her.

She almost ran into the idol, or the tiki, whatever it was.

On this side of the atoll, facing toward the lagoon, was a terribly weatherworn wooden idol, hacked from a palm tree by the look of it. The paint was faded on it, but the great big eyes were unmistakable, as were the tentacles, which had been carved vertically, making the thing look like it was flowing out of the ground.

It looked very old to her.

Paige reached out and touched the idol, felt the roughness of the wood. She could not be sure who put it there, whether it was a relic from some Pacific Islanders, or whether a half-crazed hippy castaway had made it.

She looked out into the lagoon, could see no sign of the monster. Determined, she pressed on, wanting to travel the entire length of the atoll.

It did get rougher on this side of Palmer, with ever-thicker copses of palms and other trees, all crowding what remained a narrow strip of land. She didn't know how much longer Palmer would remain above sea level, and felt some odd kinship with these trees fighting for their lives in this place, doomed to one day be drowned by the oncoming, uncaring ocean. All of this lush life would be taken away, and there wasn't a thing that anybody could do about it. The palms had landed here as coconuts long ago.

Palmer itself had begun as a volcano, sometime long ago, birthed in fire and steam, and had risen at a time she could only guess. The fires had moved on, and the earth that remained was slowly, inevitably being consumed by a ravenous sea.

Even islands weren't immune to entropy. Somehow, Paige took a bleak comfort in that, as she fought her way through the trees, searching for something, anything she might use against the octopus, to reach the *Affinity*, and, she hoped, sanctuary.

She was about 150 yards from the end of the atoll, navigating another break in the narrow jungle when she saw the catamaran gliding into the lagoon. It was a small one, with a bright orange sail, but it was unmistakably there, with outriggers.

Paige felt hope and elation, called out, wanted to cheer.

"Ahoy!" Paige said, trying to yell over the crash of the surf. She splashed toward the catamaran, almost forgetting that she had to stay away from the lagoon.

She saw two people on the catamaran, a young man and a young woman. The man was at the tiller, was piloting carefully, moving the catamaran up near the *Affinity*, and there was a woman at the bow of the catamaran, in a life vest, wearing a turquoise bikini that contrasted with her tan body.

"Hey!" Paige said.

The woman, who was wearing aviator shades, turned her gaze in the direction of Paige, waved to her.

Paige didn't know how to warn them without sounding like a crazy woman.

"Look out below," Paige said, gesturing. The woman, confused, just waved again, pointed to *Affinity*.

Paige jumped up and down, pointing into the lagoon.

She saw a tentacle rise out of the water in the wake of the catamaran, and slap against the man, wrapping him around the face. This was concealed from the woman by the great sail of the boat. With an effortless yank, the octopus pulled the man over backwards, drawing him down into the water and out of sight.

Paige pointed, screaming.

The young woman still couldn't see, was stepping uncertainly on the bow of the catamaran, which was now moving on its own, without guidance. It lurched to one side as the wind shifted, and, without the man to guide it, started to capsize, listing hard to one side as it hit the edge of the lagoon.

"No no no," Paige said. "Oh, God, no. Please. No."

It wasn't fair. It just wasn't fair.

The young woman jumped overboard, landing in the lagoon itself, was swimming for the shore, while the catamaran went over, its hull shiny and visible to Paige from where she stood.

Paige took out her asthma inhaler and took a preparatory puff, pocketed it, then dove into the water, swimming hard for the *Affinity*. It was a desperate move, but success or failure could hinge on one's willingness or failure to act in a situation. Seth had frozen; Paige would not.

Right now, the kraken was chomping on that woman's partner, was momentarily occupied with that, and she didn't know how long that would take. Maybe long enough for her to reach *Affinity*.

She would find out, she supposed, swimming freestyle for the ketch, harder than she'd ever done in her entire life.

While she did this, the woman was splashing toward the shore, calling out the name of her boyfriend.

"Dean," she said. "Dean? Dean! Where are you?"

She sounded Australian, perhaps. Paige wasn't sure, could not afford to care in that moment, swimming for the *Affinity*.

She could not allow herself to be afraid, would not do it. She hoped that the kraken was too happy to have found some more prey to be too concerned about her swimming for her life in that moment.

Paige reached the ketch and swam around to the diving platform on the back, pulled herself aboard and then scuttled up the rope ladder, actually crying as she scaled it, throwing herself into the comforting confines of *Affinity*, gasping, running up the ladder into the wheelhouse, where the radio was.

She didn't know where the EPIRB would be, but she could recognize a radio.

Paige glanced in the direction of the catamaran, saw that the woman had, in fact, made it to shore, was calling out for her boyfriend. The catamaran had gone fully over, was now upside down, the hull cooking in the sun. She thought the kraken must have overturned that boat, because she'd never seen a boat capsize so readily.

Paige didn't really understand how to use the radio, just took the microphone and pressed the talk button, and started talking.

"Mayday, mayday, mayday, this is *Affinity* at Palmer Atoll. Mayday. To any ships in the area, mayday. This is *Affinity* at Palmer Atoll, bearing 10° 28' N 170° 07' W. We need immediate assistance. Mayday. Over."

She saw the kraken emerge from the depths below her. From her vantage point in the wheelhouse, she could see it lurking, its eyes on her, tentacles splayed out.

Paige also saw the woman, who had not yet seen the beast, as it was screened from her view by the overturned catamaran.

Then Paige pointed to it, screamed for her attention and pointed. "Get away from the lagoon!"

"What?" the woman said.

"Get away from the goddamned lagoon!"

She pointed emphatically, and the woman saw it, gasped.

The kraken swam around *Affinity*, dwarfing it. She was a big boat, but the kraken was massive by comparison.

The radio crackled, somebody speaking in a language Paige could not understand.

"Mayday, mayday, mayday, this is *Affinity* at Palmer Atoll. 10° 28' N 170° 07' W. We require immediate aid. Send help. Over."

Two tentacles shot out of the water, one smacking against the windscreen in the wheelhouse, the other reaching for Paige.

The woman onshore, seeing this, screamed.

Paige dodged the tentacle, threw herself back down to the main deck, then dove belowdecks into the living quarters, throwing open the door and slamming it shut on one of the kraken's tentacles, which had been snaking after her.

The monstrous thing, smelling of seawater, flailed and turned, would not let her fully shut the door. In fact, as she threw her weight against the door, the tentacle found one of her arms and coiled around it. She felt the suckers latch onto her, these cold, wet things that were both firm and fibrous to the touch, and also strangely supple. They found her skin and she could feel the suction as they latched onto her.

Paige yelped, seeing the tapered tip of that tentacle coil up her forearm, could feel the strength of the octopus as it pulled on her, tried to get her out of the cabin. As she strained against the door, she could see through one of the *Affinity*'s portholes, could see the great barred yellow eye of the octopus peering in, looking at her.

Screaming, Paige, fought to free herself, throwing every bit of weight she had available to her against that door, refusing to let the thing pull her out of there.

The tentacle was both impossibly strong and also oddly rubbery. It was like fighting a firehose. She strained and kicked hard at the door, and between one of the kicks, the octopus released her and the tentacle whipped out of view, allowing Paige the opportunity to slam the door shut at last, locking it.

She instinctively backed away from the door, going to the far side of the boat, crying, gasping. Her asthma was making it hard to breathe, turning her breaths into horrible wheezes. She reached into her pocket and took out her rescue inhaler, took a couple of puffs on it, feeling the bronchodilator work on her worn-out lungs, making it easier for her to breathe.

The octopus was still watching her at the porthole, and she could see its suckers clamped against the boat on some of the other portholes as well.

It was an odd contrast for her, the luxurious appointments inside the cabin of *Affinity*, contrasted with the monstrosity just outside, and Paige, looking every bit the sunbleached castaway, catching her breath as she stared down the kraken.

Affinity was a prototype, an experimental boat, designed for and capable of transoceanic transit, but she was, most of all, a pleasure boat, and had been designed accordingly. As such, the wheelhouse was not fully enclosed above them. She had been designed for the helmsman to fully feel the sea, to see and hear as much as they could, to enjoy the silence of her mode of travel.

As such, it presented a problem for Paige. Not that she was well-versed enough in piloting a boat to be able to leave this lagoon with assurance—that was its own set of challenges—but rather, to do so, she would have to climb abovedecks and risk exposing herself to that creature again.

She did not want to do that. Down here, in the cabin, she had food and water and safety. With the batteries charged, she could run for a long time, she presumed, and just hope someone rescued her.

But there was the problem of the woman on the beach. Paige could not simply hunker in her bunker and leave that woman to her fate. She had to do something about it.

The kraken let go of *Affinity*, vanished from view. Paige could feel the shift of weight as it released the boat.

Paige looked at her arm, could see the red rings traveling up it, welts from where the octopus had grabbed her. It looked like some kind of odd fractal tattoo.

She would help the woman, but first, Paige had to help herself. She went to the fridge in the galley and she opened it, made herself a ham, turkey, and Havarti club sandwich, opened another bottle of champagne, drank from the bottle, sat in the galley, turned on the air conditioning, and took a breather.

The a/c was, of course, a waste of battery power in this situation, but she'd felt that she earned it, welcomed that bit of creature comfort, which felt heavenly, despite her sunburn. As she ate, she looked around her. There was an axe battened down over one of the rafters, red-handled, satisfyingly savage. An axe would do nicely.

Finishing her sandwich, drinking her champagne, Paige walked around the cabin. She had reasonable familiarity with it, since she'd been down here sick since they'd left Hawaii. She opened one of the cupboards and took out their rescue kit, found what she was looking for, the flare pistol, and put that out on the table.

There were other things aboard, too. She understood this. Sebastian was always prepared. There was storage beneath the beds and benches, and she opened everything, found what she'd wanted: a sawed-off shotgun.

She thought that would get the kraken's attention. At least she dearly hoped that it would. Taking it out, she turned it this way and that. It was a pump-action 12-gauge shotgun, and still had the stock. But the barrel was stubby. She took out two boxes of shells. One was a box of slugs, the other, 00 buckshot. What would work against the kraken?

She opted for the slugs, felt that given the kraken's rubbery consistency and carpetlike configuration, thought that buckshot would dissipate the force too much. She wanted to punch holes in the thing, and, to her, at least, that meant using slugs.

Paige loaded the shotgun, put five shells into it, cocked it, set it on the counter.

There was also a knife, a nice diving knife with a black and dayglo yellow handle. She strapped that onto her ankle.

She would take care of things, one way or another. She wanted to rest, but had to at least risk going abovedecks to see if the woman was still alive. If the kraken had gotten her, Paige would hide out below, try to wait the thing out.

Paige slung the shotgun over her back, took the axe in hand, figuring that she'd have a better chance with the axe against the tentacles than trying to blast them with the shotgun.

She went to the door, pressed her ear to it, but heard nothing.

Then Paige opened the door just a crack, listened again. Nothing.

She opened it a little wider. Nothing.

Wider still. Nothing.

Peering out, she saw no trace of the monster. Then she crept up, feeling the champagne warming her tummy, as well as the crushing tropical humidity and heat, more pronounced, now, having felt some of the air-conditioned comfort of *Affinity* once more.

"Lady of the catamaran, are you out there?" Paige called.

"Monica," the woman said, calling from somewhere on the atoll. "What is that thing?"

"It's an octopus," Paige said. "A big, hungry one. It likes to play. Welcome to Palmer Atoll, Monica. My name is Paige."

As she spoke, she crept up the steps, hands on the axe, senses attuned for any sign of the thing. Her forearm throbbed where the thing had grabbed her.

"Where's Dean?" Monica said.

"Dean's dead," Paige said. "It ate him, I promise you that."

"I see his lifejacket," Monica said.

"Stay out of the lagoon," Paige said. "It likes it there. It's the thing's lair."

The woman started crying, but Paige was too alert to otherwise pay attention to that. If that thing so much as reached for her, she'd chop off one of its arms. See what it thought of that.

"How long have you been here?"

"A few days," Paige said. "It killed the rest of my crew."

The radio crackled above, but Paige couldn't decipher it. She hoped that somebody who spoke English had heard her distress call.

"Where are you from?" Paige asked.

"Wellington," Monica said. "Our boat was the *Feisty*. Dean was taking us to Hawaii, but thought we'd see some of the atolls out here."

Paige got to the main deck, could see around her. She saw Monica was near the shelter.

"Look," Paige said. "That thing can reach you there, if you get too close to the lagoon. Try to always stay as far from the lagoon as you're able."

"Okay," Monica said. She was pretty, had brown hair and a baby face, was still wearing her life jacket. "What are we going to do?'"

"There's plenty of water in that cistern," Paige said. "You can drink your fill. You can see the coconuts I piled up there. You can eat those."

Monica's face went to horror. "You're not marooning me here, are you?"

"No," Paige said. "No, I'm just telling you what you have there, so you can survive."

She looked around, saw no sign of the beast. It was midafternoon, and the sun was beating down on them. Maybe the kraken was resting.

"There's a treehouse in that first grove," Paige said. "Just a plank, really, nailed up there. If you climb up there, the thing can't reach you."

Monica turned and looked out at the grove. "I can't see it."

"It's there," Paige said. "But you have to be very careful. The thing loves to hunt along that grove, so be very careful if you go over there."

Paige was not comfortable piloting a boat like this, frankly, but at this point, was willing to risk it rather than linger longer in the lagoon.

"Monica," Paige said. "I'm going to get the boat out of the lagoon. Now, that will mean bringing the boat relatively close to the shack. There's no good anchorage there, so I'd have to pass it by, but we'd be passing close, and you could make a run for it, could try to jump aboard."

Monica looked like she was athletic. Paige felt fairly confident that she'd be able to do that, if she were able to actually pilot *Affinity* properly.

"What kind of boat is that, anyway?" Monica asked.

"An experimental one," Paige said.

"The masts are what drew Dean in," Monica said. "He saw those, wondered what they were. We got caught in that storm, and he wondered if you did, too. Poor Dean."

Monica began sobbing again, while Paige allowed herself a moment to relax, seeing no sign of the octopus. Aboard *Affinity*, everything seemed possible again. She no longer felt like a castaway. Whether or not help came for her, Paige felt some solace in at least having made it this far.

"That thing lairs in the lagoon, like I said," Paige said. "I feel that if I can get you aboard *Affinity*, here, we can slip the lagoon and take to sea, and it will leave us behind."

"*Affinity* is a nice name," Monica said.

Paige felt reasonably sure she could pilot the boat, could run it on battery power, but was less confident about engaging the masts. She'd watched John and Sebastian do it, but hadn't been paying as much attention as she perhaps should have. The men had talked about it so much on the earlier part of the voyage that Paige had, she was embarrassed to recall, tuned them out. The combination of her cold and the endless engineering details of the masts shared between the men had benumbed her.

"I'm going to need your help, Monica," Paige said. "I'm going to need you to spot for me. I'm going to raise the anchor. Then, I'm going to go up into the wheelhouse, and I'm going to turn on the boat, am going to pilot it past you, where I said. While this is happening, I'm going to need you to keep a sharp eye out for the thing. If it is sneaking up on me or anything, you cry out and warn me, alright?"

"Okay," Monica said.

"It's very fast, and is very quiet," Paige said. "It's smart and sneaky."

Paige realized that she'd have to walk along the narrow gangway to get to the bow, to raise the anchor. She shuddered at this, could imagine the octopus snatching her as she crept her way along that narrow section of *Affinity*, could feel its tentacles seizing her, this sunbaked bon-bon, and dragging her into the depths, feasting on her in the cold comfort of its undersea garden.

Angry at her imagination, she pushed that grim imagery from her mind. She just had to raise the anchor. Of course, in so doing, she would surely get the monster's attention. Who knew what it was doing down there but if it saw the anchor go up, it would understand what she was up to. Maybe it would slither up the anchor chain and surprise her, yanking on it, throwing Paige overboard.

Maybe the savvier thing to do was to simply cut the anchor and slip out that way. It wasn't like she was going to leave the shelter of *Affinity* until she reached civilization. She'd happily beach the boat somewhere in Hawaii if it meant getting the hell away from the creature.

"Fucking mollusk," Paige said. She couldn't believe she was at the mercy of a mollusk, that this was what her life had come to.

Taking a deep breath, she crept across the gangway, senses attuned for any sign of anything untoward, the axe in her hand, even though it would be nearly useless from this position, it still brought her comfort.

She passed the great turbines, these wonders of engineering, which stood still, now, locked in place by some switch at the wheelhouse.

When she cleared the wheelhouse, she stepped away from the edge of the boat, walked around the turbines, headed for the bow, which had a nice little area for people to sit and enjoy the view. It was Meg's favorite part of the boat, where she'd spent the most time.

Paige moved past the white cushions toward the line that held the anchor. Looking around her once more, determining whether or not it was safe, Paige raised the axe and cut the line in two strokes of the axe, watched it slip down into the water with a splash.

Wincing, Paige waited, axe at the ready. It was late afternoon, now, the sun having taken its inevitable transit across the sky. Paige absolutely had to get out of the lagoon before nightfall, refused to spend another night on Palmer Atoll.

Monica cried out, pointed, and Paige turned, swung the axe around her instinctively.

Sure enough, there was a spray of tentacles, actually on either side of *Affinity*, six arms, three to a side, flailing and reaching for her.

Paige screamed as she felt one of the tentacles latch onto her leg, throwing her to the ground. She took a swing with the axe, missing, burying it in the deck of the boat. Having found her, the octopus yanked hard, pulling her across the deck, yanking the axe out of her hands. The port tentacle had caught her, so the starboard ones vanished from view, only to reemerge on the other side in moments.

The thing dragged her to the edge of the boat, having grabbed her through the railing along the gunwale. Two more tentacles landed on her, and Paige shuddered as they gripped her legs, hauled her to the very edge.

Paige slipped the shotgun free and blasted the tentacles at her feet, gratified by the roar of the gun and by the explosion of octopus flesh and blood at the point of impact. She cocked the shotgun again and fired another shot, severing one of the tentacles.

The other tentacles released her, and vanished from view.

Paige pried the writhing tentacle off her leg, saw the green-blue blood splashing on *Affinity*'s pristine white and wooden deck.

She let out a war whoop, raised the shotgun over her head.

"Take that, Sucker," she said, felt particularly glad that she was still alive. The tentacle was still twitching, was bigger around than her thigh, the suction cups sticking to and releasing the deck spasmodically.

Paige cocked the shotgun again, then slipped it over her shoulder, pried the axe loose of the deck, and went to the aft of the boat. She hoped the kraken was nursing its wounds, would leave them alone. How many arms did an octopus have to lose to be dissuaded from attacking? Paige was prepared to take them all, if she had to.

She hoped that losing even one of its limbs would deter the beast from making another attack on her. But she couldn't bank on it, got to the wheelhouse and turned on the engines.

With the boat pointing toward the edge of the lagoon, she threw the wheel to port, turned the boat around, and slowed the thing to a crawl, fearful of running aground if she was too hasty. She wanted to leave Palmer Atoll behind more than anything, but refused to push things too hard.

Affinity responded readily to her prodding, and she made a stately half-circle in the lagoon, until she was pointing where she needed to go, while Paige kept her eyes on where she was headed, and her ears out for Monica. One of the nicest things about *Affinity* was how quiet she was, her electric motor whirring softly, churning water and delivering her from the lagoon in style.

Monica ran to the edge of the atoll, watching *Affinity* pass, and then she took a running leap, diving into the water, swimming hard for the aft of *Affinity*. The entrance to the lagoon was a straight shot, so Paige risked looking aft, to keep an eye on things as Monica swam for her. Paige throttled down just a bit, gave Monica the chance to grab onto the diving platform, to pull herself aboard.

When she saw that she was aboard, Paige throttled up, and cruised out of the lagoon, and out onto the churning, surging sea, proud of herself at her accomplishment. Now if she could just keep them from running aground in the treacherous shoals outside of the supposed safety of the lagoon, she'd really be making progress.

Paige looked at the console, saw a pair of switches that were marked "Turbine 1" and "Turbine 2," toggled them, and she watched the turbines begin to turn, watching the wind replenishing the battery stores. They were underway, rising and falling in the waves of the Pacific.

Paige had turned on the sonar, lest any seamounts catch them by surprise, and had watched Palmer Atoll slip out of view to the east, as they sailed toward the sunset. Her goal was to head north, toward Hawaii, but she wanted to put plenty of room between her and the atoll. There were plenty of other islands, reefs, and other navigation hazards around this area, so it paid to be careful.

Monica had been overjoyed at her timely rescue, although she was still mournful about the loss of Dean. Monica's eyes were nut brown, and she was very pretty, looked to be perhaps part Asian to Paige's eyes.

She was also a capable sailor, more so than Paige. Paige entrusted her to the wheel, let her get them on a northerly heading, while Paige went amidships and picked up the tentacle, walked that down belowdecks, took out a cooler that she filled with ice, and stuffed the thing in there, then slipped that cooler into the freezer, hoping it would keep it safe.

Paige couldn't wait to show them that at the Zoological Society of Wherever—whoever took it would find themselves a real prize, and Paige imagined herself on the talk show circuit, telling the harrowing tale of survival in the South Seas. She was already crafting her memoirs in her head, regretting that she hadn't taken Seth's journal with her, but figured it belonged on the atoll, would be there for somebody else to find, and hopefully to not be caught unawares by the kraken, like had happened so many times before.

Paige had finished stowing the tentacle, had picked up a couple of beers from the fridge and was going abovedecks when she saw Monica go hurtling overhead, grabbed by a pair of tentacles.

Monica screamed, reaching for Paige, who dropped the beers and reached out for Monica. She actually caught the woman with her right hand, Monica half-on, half-off the boat.

Monica was screaming, veins sticking out on her forehead as she and Paige strained against the pull of the thing.

"Oh God, oh God, you said it would stay in the lagoon," Monica said. "You said!"

Paige drew the diving knife with her free hand, although she was bracing against the side of the boat with her legs, using every bit of strength she had not to lose her grip on Monica. But the octopus was so much heavier than either of them, and was far stronger.

Three more tentacles slapped across Monica, one of them right across her pretty face. It yanked back, and Monica's neck snapped, and she went limp, slipped overboard.

Paige cried out, swinging belatedly at the tentacles that were no longer there, as Monica went into the sea with a splash.

"No," Paige said. "Goddammit, no."

The water churned as the sun set, and darkness fell. Paige was terrified to be up in the wheelhouse after dark, so she ran up and shut off the engine, would let them drift.

Then she ran down belowdecks, locked herself into the cabin, cried. She hadn't even had time to get to know the poor woman. She really had thought they were safe, that once they cleared that monster's lair, that would be that.

Paige went to one of the bunks and collapsed on it, crying. It wasn't fair. She'd beaten the thing. Why had it kept after them? She wondered if, smart as it was, would it have wanted some kind of revenge on her for having taken one of its limbs.

There was no way of knowing.

She really had thought they were safe.

—

FIVE

AFFINITY was found 45 days later, adrift off the coast of Molokai, without anyone aboard. There were shotgun blasts on the deck, and an axe was buried in the side of the boat, at the gunwale. The Titan Electric Boat recovery team had found her to otherwise be in good condition, and had discovered a few curiosities—there was a great tentacle found in the freezer, which marine zoologists had later identified as *Enteroctopus giganteas,* a hitherto undiscovered giant octopus.

A lone journal entry was found, scrawled on a sheet of paper, pinned to the galley counter with a steak knife:

SEPTEMBER 23, 2012

Full moon tonight. The kraken followed us out. I didn't think it would do that, thought it would be content to stay in its home. After all that happened, I didn't think it would do that. I'm going to kill the fucking thing. One way or another, it's ending tonight. I'm hoping with the light of the moon, it'll help me see it better. I think it's clinging to the bottom of the ship, nursing its wounds, waiting for me to lower my guard.

It killed Monica. It killed Dean. It killed Meg. It killed Sebastian. It killed John. It killed Seth. It killed Ron. It killed Angela. It killed hundreds more.

But it's not going to kill me, because I'm a survivor.

Until next time,
Paige Wilkins

THE END

ACKNOWLEDGMENTS

I would like to thank all of my readers, who offered their time, attention, and opinions to the writing and revision of this novella. I would also like to thank Christine Marie Scott of Clever Crow Design Studio in Pittsburgh for her wonderful cover art and her invaluable assistance with the layout of these pages.

ABOUT THE AUTHOR

D. T. Neal is a fiction writer and editor living in Chicago. He won second place in the Aeon Award in 2008 for his short story, "Aegis," and has been published in *Albedo 1,* Ireland's premier magazine of science fiction, horror, and fantasy. He is the author of *Saamaanthaa* and *The Happening,* both part of the Wolfshadow Trilogy. He's also written the vampire novel, *Suckage,* as well as the Lovecraftian cosmic horror-thriller, *Chosen.* He has written two creature feature/eco-horror novellas, *Relict* and *Summerville.* He continues to work on several science fiction, fantasy, horror, and thriller stories.

DTNEAL.COM

ALSO BY D.T. NEAL

Saamaanthaa

The Happening

Suckage

Chosen

Summerville

N✱P

NOSETOUCH PRESS

Nosetouch Press is an independent book publisher tandemly-based in Chicago and Pittsburgh. We are dedicated to bringing some of today's most energizing fiction to readers around the world.

Our commitment to classic book design in a digital environment brings an innovative and authentic approach to the traditions of literary excellence.

✱The Nose Knows™
NOSETOUCHPRESS.COM

Horror | Science Fiction | Fantasy | Mystery | Supernatural

Printed in Great Britain
by Amazon